IGGY LOOMIS

A HAGFISH CALLED SHIRLEY

JENNIFER ALLISON

⋯ Illustrated by MIKE MORAN ⋯

DIAL BOOKS FOR YOUNG READERS An imprint of Penguin Group (USA) LLC

DIAL BOOKS FOR YOUNG READERS
Published by the Penguin Group • Penguin Group (USA) LLC
375 Hudson Street • New York, New York 10014

USA | Canada | UK | Ireland | Australia | New Zealand | India | South Africa | China
penguin.com

A PENGUIN RANDOM HOUSE COMPANY

Library of Congress Cataloging-in-Publication Data
Allison, Jennifer.
A hagfish called Shirley / by Jennifer Allison ; illustrated by Mike Moran.
pages cm — (Iggy Loomis ; book #2)
Summary: "When Iggy flushes a pet down the toilet, Daniel has to convince him to use his
alien powers to save the day and keep everyone out of trouble"— Provided by publisher.
ISBN 978-0-8037-3781-5 (hardback)
[1. Brothers—Fiction. 2. Family life—Fiction. 3. Fishes—Fiction. 4. Extraterrestrial beings—Fiction.
5. Mutation (Biology)—Fiction. 6. Science fiction.] I. Title.
PZ7.A4428Hag 2014 [Fic]—dc23   2014010763

1 3 5 7 9 10 8 6 4 2

Designed by Jason Henry • Text set in Napoleone Slab

To Max, Marcus, and Gigi,
my favorite book lovers and pet owners!
–J.A.

To Kristin
–M.M.

· 1 ·

FLYING IGGY

"**I CAN'T WAIT TO SEE** Awistair's new pet!" my little brother, Iggy, shouted.

Iggy was super-excited because Alistair had just called to say that he had caught some kind of "amazing creature," and that we should come over to see it right away. As we walked to Alistair's house next door, Iggy kept running back and forth across the sidewalk and nearly crashing into me each time he passed.

"Alistair doesn't have a new *pet,* Iggy," I said. "It's probably a creature he's studying—one of his science projects."

Alistair is always catching all kinds of insects and bugs and observing them in his home laboratory, so I figured this new creature he wanted to show us was also one of his "specimens." Whatever it was, Alistair was very excited about it. *"You've never seen anything like this before!"* he had practically shouted over the phone.

"Maybe Awistair get a monkey!" Iggy said.

"I doubt it, Iggy," I said, although I secretly thought that if there was anyone in my neighborhood who *could* get a pet monkey, it would probably be Alistair.

"I HOPE AWISTAIR GET A MONKEY!" Iggy jumped up and hung from a tree branch, then swung from it with his feet dangling over the sidewalk.

"Cut it out, Iggy!" When Iggy gets too excited, it's just a matter of time before something goes wrong.

"Or maybe Awistair get a toowantoowa!" Iggy hoisted his feet up and over the tree branch like an acrobat.

"You mean *tarantula*," I said, watching Iggy walk along the tree branch as if it were a balance beam.

Uh-oh, I thought, holding my breath. *What dumb move was Iggy going to make next?!*

Iggy paused and then scampered farther up the trunk of the tree like a large squirrel. (By now, you've probably noticed that my little brother isn't the average preschooler.)

"IGGY!" I shouted up into the tree branches. "GET BACK DOWN HERE, AND I MEAN IT!"

Leaves rustled. I heard giggling, but I couldn't see Iggy.

I glanced around to see if any of our neighbors had noticed Iggy up in the tree. (Alistair and I are the only kids who know the truth about Iggy, and it isn't easy to keep everyone, including my parents, from finding out our secret.)

"IGGY!" I shouted again. "IF YOU DON'T GET DOWN FROM THERE RIGHT NOW, I'M GOING TO ALISTAIR'S HOUSE WITHOUT YOU, AND YOU WON'T GET TO SEE ALISTAIR'S NEW ANIMAL THAT'S PROBABLY A MONKEY!!"

That got Iggy's attention.

"WAIT FOR ME, DANO!!" Iggy burst out from the tree branches and into the sky, like a giant bird. He had sprouted giant dragonfly wings!

I tried not to panic as I watched Iggy soar through the air. I had seen him do this before, and I always worried that he might fall.

As it turned out, Iggy seemed to know exactly how to use his dragonfly wings. I breathed a sigh of relief as I watched my little brother glide gently down to the sidewalk.

· 2 ·

BUG BOY

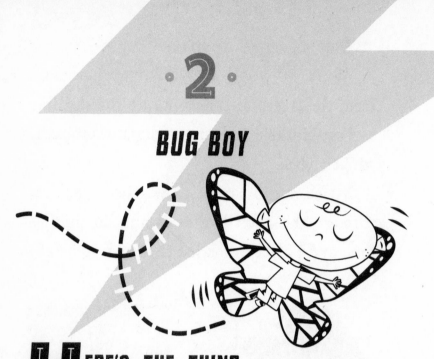

HERE'S THE THING about my little brother, Iggy: Whenever he gets either super-angry or way too excited about something, weird changes happen. Basically, his body starts growing insect parts, like wings, antennae, stingers, and even little bug fangs or claws.

The worst part is that there's no way to predict which insect traits will pop out each time he changes.

Sometimes Iggy becomes part ladybug or butterfly. . . .

Sometimes Iggy is part wasp, yellow jacket, or honeybee.

Sometimes Iggy is part mosquito, ant, flea, or housefly.

And sometimes—like now—he becomes part dragonfly.

And whenever Iggy's bug traits pop out, I have to give him his "Human Normalizer" to turn him back to a regular human kid before anyone notices.

What, you ask, is the Human Normalizer?

It looks like an ordinary pacifier, but it does something amazing: It turns Iggy back into a regular kid after he starts changing into a bug boy.

"Here, Iggy," I said, sticking the Human Normalizer into his mouth as I glanced around once more to make sure nobody had seen his dragonfly wings. "Get calm before someone sees those wings of yours."

With the Human Normalizer in his mouth, Iggy sat at the foot of the tree and closed his eyes. I watched his dragonfly wings grow smaller until they disappeared.

"Come on, Iggy," I said, after Iggy had rested for a few minutes. "Time to go to Alistair's house."

Iggy rubbed his eyes and nodded. "Awistair get a monkey!" he said as he marched up the steps to Alistair's front door.

ALISTAIR'S ANIMALS

BEFORE WE COULD even knock, Alistair appeared in the doorway. "I thought you'd never get here!" he said, even though we had just talked on the phone about fifteen minutes ago. Alistair is usually pretty calm and quiet, but today he seemed way more excited than usual.

"Hurry!" Alistair said, leading Iggy and me down the hallway toward his room. "She can't wait to meet you!"

"*Who* can't wait to meet us?" I asked.

Alistair didn't answer; he just led to his room, which looks more like a weird science lab than a regular kid's bedroom.

He has tanks and containers of all sizes filled with things like beetles, slugs, ladybugs, centipedes, hermit crabs, frogs, and snails.

"YOU SO LUCKY-DUCK, AWISTAIR!" Iggy shouted as he ran around Alistair's room, looking at all the creatures. "YOU GOTS SO MANY PETS!"

Lately, Iggy and his twin sister, Dottie, have been begging our parents for a pet, but

Mom and Dad just say, "If it poops or needs to be fed, *the answer is no!*"

"I WISH-TED I CAN KEEP ALL DESE ANIMOS!" Iggy shouted, still running around Alistair's room.

"Iggy, if you like those life-forms," said Alistair, "wait until you see *this* one!" Alistair pulled away a sheet that covered a large glass aquarium. "Ta-da! Meet Shirley!"

A snake-like creature twisted itself in coils at the sandy bottom of the tank.

"*That's* Shirley?!" I don't know what I was expecting, but I guess the name "Shirley" made me picture something a little cuter.

"WOW!" Iggy ran to the tank and pressed his face against the glass. "What dat snake doing?"

"It isn't a snake," Alistair said. "Shirley is a hagfish."

I squinted into the aquarium. "She doesn't look like any fish I've seen before."

"Exactly!" said Alistair. "If you could combine a fish and a worm into one creature, you might get something like Shirley."

"You mean, you created her?" I pictured Alistair using his lab equipment to combine a fish and a worm into one completely new animal. From what I knew about Alistair's science experiments, it was the sort of thing he might actually be able to do.

"Daniel, I don't go around making new life-forms! You know that's against the rules."

Are you sure about that, Alistair? I thought, glancing at Iggy.

"Hagfishes live at the bottom of the ocean," Alistair continued. "Last weekend, my parents took me to the beach, and I decided to do some scuba diving. That's where I found Shirley."

I'm used to hearing about the amazing things Alistair can do, so I wasn't even too surprised about his "undersea expedition."

"So you caught this thing," I said, pointing at the hagfish, "and then you decided to name it *Shirley*?!" For some reason, I just couldn't get past that name.

Alistair smiled into the tank and waved at Shirley. "I thought she looked like a Shirley. Isn't she cute?"

Shirley wiggled the tentacle-whiskers around her funnel-shaped mouth. If you ask me, she was the opposite of cute. *But maybe she looks cute to Alistair,* I thought.

After all, I reminded myself, *Alistair isn't human.*

ALISTAIR'S BIG SECRET

I'M GOING TO LET YOU IN on a huge secret, okay?

Alistair and his parents are actually aliens from a distant planet called Blaron. All three members of his family *look* completely human on the outside, but it's just a disguise. Their *true* form looks more like something related to a squid or maybe an octopus, only way bigger and a whole lot weirder. Believe me, it's not a pretty sight. In fact, when you consider what the average Blaronite looks like, I guess it makes sense that Alistair thinks Shirley is "cute."

ALISTAIR DISGUISED AS A HUMAN

ALISTAIR IN HIS NATURAL (BLARONITE) FORM

I'm the only human who knows the whole truth about Alistair's alien identity. I mean, Iggy and Dottie know that Alistair can travel to a place called "Planet Blaron"—in fact, Iggy's even been there himself—but grown-ups never really believe the weird stuff preschoolers say.

"But if *anyone else* discovers that aliens have been living right here in their own neighborhood," Alistair once told me, "my family could either end up dead or locked in some government laboratory."

I hated the idea of losing my best friend, so I promised Alistair I'd help keep his true identity a secret.

Of course, I had no idea how complicated things were going to get after Iggy met that hagfish called Shirley.

· 5 ·

SPEAKING OF INTESTINES . . .

"WHAT DEY EATS?"** Iggy pressed his nose against the glass hagfish tank.

"They eat whatever they find dead at the bottom of the ocean," Alistair said, pointing to the hagfish's mouth, which was shaped like a funnel. "Instead of regular teeth, Shirley has rows of sharp rasps that she uses to gnaw a hole through the surface of the fish. Then she crawls inside and eats the animal from the inside out."

Tentacles for sensing though smell and touch

Funnel Mouth (No jaw)

Eye Spot

Rasp (teeth)

Alistair explained all of this in a happy tone of voice, as if he were telling us how Shirley enjoys licking lollipops and chocolate ice-cream cones.

Next, Alistair told us how Shirley is "practically blind."

1. Whitish hagfish eye-spots with no pupils (mostly blind)

He explained how she uses the tentacle things on her head to smell and touch her surroundings:

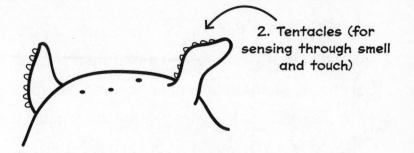

2. Tentacles (for
sensing through smell
and touch)

And then he explained how Shirley "absorbs nutrition through her skin."

3. Hagfish skin absorbs
nutrients without even
taking a bite!

"Speaking of ice cream and intestines," Alistair said, "I should feed Shirley now."

Alistair removed the lid from Shirley's aquarium. He reached down into the water and gently grasped the squirming hagfish. "It's okay, Shirley," Alistair said. "It's just me."

"I want hode Haggie!" Iggy jumped up and down and reached for the hagfish as eagerly as if it were a kitten or a puppy.

"You can hold Shirley after she's had her

lunch." After putting Shirley back in her aquarium, Alistair opened a container packed with ice and tossed a very large, dead fish into the hagfish tank. Shirley jumped onto that fish so fast you would have thought it was a delicious cheeseburger.

We watched as Shirley gnawed a hole into the side of the dead fish, then wriggled her way inside her dinner until we couldn't see her anymore. Now all we could see was a dead fish, flopping around at the bottom of the tank.

"See?" said Alistair. "Shirley's eating the trout from the inside now."

For some reason, I felt a little queasy watching that dead trout twitching around with Shirley gnawing on its insides. I guess I had a gut feeling that something was about to go wrong.

THE BEST PET EVER

"**H**AGGIE ALL DONE wif lunch!" Iggy announced, pointing to the aquarium, where Shirley swam through the bones of the fish she had just eaten. "NOW I hode Haggie!"

"You can hold Shirley if you're *very careful*," Alistair said.

Iggy nodded. "I touch Haggie *gently*."

Alistair scooped Shirley into a net then dropped her into a plastic bucket filled with water. "Iggy, if you want to hold Shirley, you have to go stand in the bathtub, okay? The carpet in this room will get ruined if you try to hold her in here."

I thought it was a little unusual for Alistair to worry about his carpet getting ruined since he keeps so many weird creatures, not to mention gooey chemicals in his room, but I didn't say anything. Iggy and I followed Alistair from his bedroom to the bathroom across the hallway.

"Okay, Iggy," Alistair said. "Now climb into the bathtub."

"Oh boy!" Iggy eagerly climbed into the bathtub. "I going hode Haggie!!"

Alistair reached into the bucket and gently grasped the hagfish. "Take it easy, Shirley," Alistair said. "I'm right here. It's your buddy, Alistair."

I had never heard Alistair use phrases like "*Take it easy*" and "*It's your buddy, Alistair.*" Owning a hagfish seemed to bring out a whole different side to his personality. I guess he seemed more *human.*

Alistair lifted the squirming hagfish from the tank. "It's okay, girl. Iggy is going to hold you for just a minute."

Iggy jumped up and down and clapped his hands with excitement.

"Be careful, Iggy," Alistair warned. "Whatever you do, *don't drop her!*"

"Okay!"

Holding Shirley, Iggy looked as if he had just received the biggest Christmas present of his life.

But then something really strange and incredibly gross happened: thick slime poured from the hagfish's skin in long, gluey sheets.

"WHOA! HO HO HO!" Iggy was thrilled with the hagfish slime. *"Haggie blowded his noses wif eleventy-sixty boogers!!"*

"That is *a lot* of slime," I said.

It was hard to believe that all that slime came from one animal. All I can say is, if you're the kind of person who wants to own the slimiest pet in the world, a hagfish might be the one for you.

"It's *mucus*, not slime," Alistair said, correcting me.

"It's very slimy mucus," I replied.

Iggy's face was one big smile. His shirt was covered in hagfish slime. "Look, Dano!" he said proudly. "Haggie like me!"

"It doesn't necessarily mean that she *likes* you," Alistair replied. "That mucus is how Shirley *defends* herself."

Alistair told us all about hagfish slime.

If a shark tries to eat a hagfish . . .

The hagfish's skin releases thick mucus that clogs the shark's gills so it can't breathe.

HA-HA! SERVES YOU RIGHT!

The shark chokes, and the hagfish escapes!

"So in other words, Shirley's trying to slime you to death, Iggy," I teased.

Iggy's eyes grew wide.

"Exactly," said Alistair, very seriously. "Hagfish slime is a very *effective* defensive weapon."

"OH, DAT SO AWESOME, AWISTAIR! I GOING USE DIS HAGGIE FOR A WEAPON WHEN WE PLAY HIDE-AND-SEEK—"

"No, Iggy," Alistair said. "Shirley is NOT a weapon. She's . . . She's . . ."

"She's *what*?" I asked.

Alistair's face broke into a smile. "She's my *pet!*"

Alistair seemed so surprised and happy about the idea of having a pet; I figured the whole idea must be new to him.

But then Alistair's smile disappeared as if he suddenly remembered something that worried him. "I mean—" he said. "I just hope—"

"Dano!" Iggy interrupted. "Tell Mom to get me one haggie pet for my berfday, okay? Dis da best pet I ever seed!"

"Iggy, there's no way Mom will ever get you a pet hagfish," I told him.

"YES, MOM WILL GET ME ONE HAGGIE FOR MY BERFDAY!!" Iggy shouted, his face turning red.

Uh-oh, I thought. Iggy was gearing up to throw a huge tantrum.

Alistair caught my eye, and I knew what he was thinking: *We might have a bug boy on our hands any minute now!*

· 7 ·

SOMETHING UNEXPECTED

"SHIRLEY WANTS TO GO** back to her bucket now, Iggy," Alistair said, reaching for his pet hagfish and trying not to upset Iggy. "Shirley's a little scared."

"NO!" Iggy wasn't about to hand Shirley back without a struggle.

I grabbed for the hagfish. "Put that hagfish back right now!"

But Iggy was too fast for me. He sprung up from the bathtub and gripped the bathroom ceiling using one of the bug traits that sometimes pops out when he's angry: fingers that can stick to anything like Super Glue.

Alistair and I stared up at Iggy. He gripped the ceiling with one hand and hung onto Shirley with the other.

"Easy there, Iggy," said Alistair, in the same patient voice he had used with Shirley. "Let's gently release Shirley into this nice bucket of water, where she'll be safe."

"Quit acting dumb, Iggy, and just give the hagfish back!" I blurted.

I should know by now that yelling at Iggy only makes him act crazier, but sometimes I just can't help it.

"NO!!" Iggy tried to swing himself away from us, but the hagfish slipped from his hand.

Alistair lunged to catch Shirley in his bucket . . .

Unfortunately, Alistair missed.

Shirley fell into the toilet!

Everything happened so quickly: We were all shouting as Shirley wriggled and splashed in the toilet bowl.

The next thing I knew, Iggy had dropped down from the ceiling and before Alistair or I could stop him, he reached for Shirley. But instead of pulling Shirley out of the toilet, Iggy did something so incredibly dumb, Alistair and I could hardly believe what had just happened.

Iggy flushed Alistair's pet hagfish down the toilet!

THE POO-POO PARTY

Bye-bye, Haggie!

AFTER WAVING GOOD-BYE to the hagfish, Iggy clapped for himself. "I WIN!" he shouted.

Alistair just stared into the toilet. I think he was in shock.

I was about to yell at Iggy, but then I reminded myself how that would probably make more of his bug traits pop out, which was the last thing we needed.

"Haggie swim down to da poo-poo party," Iggy said, pointing at the toilet.

"'The poo-poo party?'" Alistair's neck looked blotchy. He stared at me, demanding an explanation. *"The poo-poo party?!"*

"It's a story my mom told Iggy when he was first getting potty trained," I explained.

"Come back now, Haggie-Baby!" Iggy called into the toilet.

Alistair looked totally confused as I tried to explain how, when Iggy was first learning to use the potty, he kept saying his poops were "too scared" to be flushed down the toilet. Then I told Alistair how my mom came up with the idea of telling Iggy that "all the poops get to go to a fun poo-poo party under the city," hoping that Iggy wouldn't be scared anymore.

"But that isn't true," Alistair said. "There's no party under the city. Your mom lied!"

"Human parents do that sometimes, Alistair," I told him.

"They do?! But human parents tell kids *not* to lie!" he yelled.

"Well," I said, "my mom only lied about the poo-poo party because she wanted to help Iggy get potty trained."

I couldn't blame Alistair for feeling confused. I remembered feeling pretty confused myself when I first overheard that weird poo-poo-party conversation between Iggy and my mom.

"Is the poo-poo party a berfday party for poops?" Iggy had asked.

"Um, okay," Mom had said. "I suppose it's kind of like a birthday party."

"Can I go to dat berfday party, too?"

"No, Iggy," said Mom. "It's only a party for poops."

"But my poops is scared to go to dat party. Dey wants me to come wif dem."

"They aren't scared, Iggy," Mom said. "It's *fun* for them to get flushed down the toilet to the party."

"Will dey have cake?"

I guess Mom wasn't expecting *that* question because she didn't say anything for a minute.

"Dey wants *cake!*" Iggy insisted.

"Okay," Mom said in a small voice. I think she realized she had dug herself into a hole with this poo-poo-party thing.

"And dey wants a swimming pool, too," Iggy said.

As it turned out, Mom thought she was a genius because her poo-poo-party idea actually worked, and Iggy got potty trained. The problem was that Iggy loved sending a whole bunch of things down to the poo-poo party, including one of his stuffed animals.

When my dad got tired of hearing Mom yell, "We need the plunger again!" he decided to tell Iggy the truth about Mom's poo-poo-party story. Dad sat Iggy down and explained that there is actually *not* a poo-poo party under our city.

But Iggy liked Mom's made-up story better, so he decided not to believe a word Dad said. No matter how many times Dad explained that *"things in the toilet go down a pipe and then into the sewer, and then into a water-treatment center, AND THEN THAT'S ALL,"* Iggy just nodded and said, "Dat where da party is!"

"So anyway," I told Alistair, "my mom's story is probably the reason Iggy wanted to flush Shirley down the toilet."

"HAAAAAGIEEEEE!" Iggy yelled into the toilet. "COME HOME NOW!"

Alistair just stared at Iggy. I figured that by now, he must be pretty disappointed in "human intelligence."

"Iggy, things that you flush down a toilet are *gone*," I said. "Alistair's hagfish can't just come running back up the pipes and into the toilet."

Iggy's lip quivered. "Haggie GONE?"

"Of course she's gone!" Alistair snapped. "YOU FLUSHED HER DOWN THE TOILET!"

Iggy's eyes grew wide with the surprise of being yelled at by the normally calm Alistair.

Uh-oh, I thought. *At any moment now, Iggy's gonna blow.*

Iggy threw his head back and howled:

"I'm sorry, Iggy," Alistair said. "I didn't mean—"

I WANT HAGGIEEE!

I tried to stick the Human Normalizer into Iggy's mouth, but he just swatted it away.

Then I remembered how Alistair has a special watch that's actually a secret alien control panel.

I had seen Alistair use his watch to turn toys into instant robots and bicycles into helicopters. *There must be some way that watch could rescue Alistair's hagfish!* I thought.

"Alistair," I said, struggling to be heard over Iggy's screams. "Can't you just push one of the alien technology buttons on your watch to get the hagfish back?"

But then I noticed that Alistair wasn't wearing his watch.

"My parents took it away," Alistair said glumly. "And I have no idea when they'll give it back."

"They took it away?! Why would they do *that*?" I had never heard of Alistair getting in trouble with his parents before.

"HAGGIE, HAGGIE, HAGGIE, HAGGIE!!" Iggy bawled. "*HAAAAAGIEEEEEEEE!*"

"It's my punishment for going off-mission and bringing home a pet hagfish without my parents' permission," Alistair explained, raising his voice to be heard over Iggy's sobbing. "My parents said, 'Your mission on Earth isn't collecting pets; it's growing frackenpoy, and that's all!' They took away the watch until I show that I'm more focused on my broccoli mission."

Ever since an environmental disaster ruined the soil on Alistair's home planet,

Alistair's Earth mission has been studying the best ways to grow broccoli, which is called "frackenpoy" in the Blaronite language. Broccoli happens to be the only food that Blaronites can digest, so Alistair spends most of his time either growing broccoli plants and researching things that affect broccoli, like insects and the weather.

"If it's not about frackenpoy, my parents aren't interested," Alistair said.

"HAGGIE!!" Iggy screamed. "COME! BACK! WIGHT! NOW!!"

I looked at Iggy and noticed something I had never seen before. Stiff, spiky hairs that resembled hairbrush bristles had popped up from Iggy's arms. I had seen Iggy sprout antennae on his forehead, wings from his shoulder blades, and a wasp stinger from his butt before, but these things were new.

"They look like caterpillar stingers," Alistair whispered. "Quick—we have to move fast!"

Before I could say anything, Alistair

grabbed Iggy and held him tightly, trying to restrain him. "Now!" Alistair hissed. "The Normalizer!"

Alistair quickly grabbed the Human Normalizer from me and tried to stick it in Iggy's mouth, but Iggy kept trying to sting Alistair with those scary-looking bristles on his arms.

It was weird that Alistair didn't seem bothered by the caterpillar stingers: "No, no, Iggy," he kept saying, as if Iggy were simply reaching for an extra cookie instead of trying to stab him with stingers.

Finally, Alistair managed to stick the Human Normalizer into Iggy's mouth, and Iggy sat down with a thud, looking a little stunned.

A second later, Iggy crawled back into the empty bathtub and curled up to rest.

"Didn't those caterpillar stingers hurt?" I asked Alistair.

To be honest, I had never even heard of caterpillars with stingers before. All I knew was that I was glad I hadn't been the one holding Iggy's wrists because those things looked as sharp as needles!

"It didn't hurt much," Alistair said. "But that's probably because Blaronites don't feel pain the same way humans do."

"I guess that's lucky," I said, trying to think of something that would cheer Alistair up after losing his hagfish.

"I suppose so." Alistair just stood there, staring at the toilet. I knew he must be thinking about his lost hagfish, and I couldn't think of a single thing to say that would make him feel better.

"Well," I finally said, "I guess it's also lucky we still have the Human Normalizer to help control Iggy even though your parents took away your watch."

Alistair nodded slowly. He seemed to be thinking very hard about something. Then he suddenly looked happier. "Daniel, you've just given me a great idea!"

"What is it?" I asked.

"Come on," Alistair said, leading me back to his room. "First, we need to find my old-fashioned tools!"

A STRANGE INVENTION

ALISTAIR'S HANDS moved quickly over wires and tiny bits of metal, gluing and snapping bits of his "old-fashioned tools" together. Every now and then he asked me to hold something while he worked.

"If my parents hadn't taken away my Blaronite watch," Alistair said, "I would create an insta-robot and program it to go down into the sewer to retrieve Shirley."

"That would be awesome!" I said, wishing I could see the insta-robot Alistair would have created. It was so annoying that Alistair's parents had taken away Alistair's watch, which happens to be the most awesome gadget in the universe!

"But since we don't have the watch, this handmade hagfish rescuer I just invented is the next-best thing."

Alistair and I stared at the strange contraption he had created, which looked like a combination of a telescope, a video camera, a laptop computer, and a fishing pole.

Alistair and I lugged the hagfish rescuer to the bathroom, where Iggy was still napping in the bathtub. I was glad to see that the caterpillar stingers had disappeared from his arms.

"So what next?" I asked.

"First, we send an underwater video camera down the pipes and into the sewer to locate Shirley," Alistair said. "Then we watch what happens on this screen."

Alistair showed me the miniature computer screen where we could monitor the action.

"DAT LOOK SO AWESOME!"

Alistair and I both turned to see Iggy sitting up in the bathtub, wide awake. You never would have known that he had been sound asleep just a second ago. That's the funny thing about Iggy: one moment he's sleeping hard as a rock; the next moment he's talking and running around as if he just drank three cups of coffee or something.

"Can I going fish wif dat computer?" Iggy asked, climbing out of the bathtub to get a closer look at Alistair's invention.

"This is not a toy, Iggy!" I said. "Alistair built this to *rescue his hagfish*. Remember? The hagfish *you flushed down the toilet?*"

Iggy nodded. "Haggie go to da berfday party in da potty," he said, as if we would be happy to be reminded of the whole poo-poo-party idea.

First, Alistair pushed a button and a small video camera moved on a long, stretchy cord, down into the toilet. Next, a fuzzy image of the murky sewer pipe appeared on Alistair's computer monitor.

"Oooooooo!" said Iggy. "Dat look scary! Poor Haggie!"

"Now for some bait." Alistair pushed a button and a fishing pole popped out of his hagfish-rescue invention.

"WHOA!" Iggy shouted. "WE GOING FISH YOU OUT NOW, HAGGIE!"

"Iggy," said Alistair, "can you get me a dead fish from Shirley's pail of food?"

Iggy saluted and raced from the bathroom.

A second later, Iggy skipped back into the bathroom waving a dead fish in the air as if it were a trophy he had just won.

"Thanks, Iggy." Alistair speared the dead fish with a hook and then flushed it down the toilet. "That's our bait to catch Shirley."

We all stared at the small computer screen, hoping to see Alistair's hagfish appear out of the dark water and take the bait.

"COME GET A SNACK, HAGGIE!" Iggy yelled into the toilet.

"She can't hear you, Iggy," I told him.

Iggy didn't care; he was jittery with excitement. "Dis so awesome, Dano!" Iggy grabbed my arm. "WE FISHING IN DA TOILET!"

I suddenly realized that "fishing in the toilet" was probably the *worst* example we could set for Iggy, who already seems to think of toilets as some kind of playground. "Don't *ever* try this at home, Iggy," I warned.

"Okay," Iggy said. "I only going potty fishing a COUPLE WHILES."

"No!" I said, "*NEVER* do this at our house."

"Hey!" Alistair said, pointing to the quivering fishing line. "I think we've got something!"

He was right! Something tugged on the line.

On the viewing screen, we saw Shirley gnawing on the bait!

Alistair pulled on the fishing pole. "I think we've got her!"

But as Alistair tried to reel in the hagfish, the fishing line wouldn't budge. "She's stronger than I expected!" Alistair gasped.

Alistair braced himself, pulling as hard as he could.

I watched Alistair trying to reel in his hagfish, while Iggy pulled on Alistair's waist.

They pulled and pulled!

"I think . . . we've almost got her . . ." Alistair gasped.

But just as we were about to reel in the hagfish, there was an angry knock on the door.

"Alistair?"

It was Alistair's mom, and she sounded worried.

"What's going on in there?"

It was Alistair's dad, and he sounded angry.

"Open the door, Alistair! We need to talk to you!"

Alistair's parents usually spend their time working in their broccoli garden and not bothering Alistair, so it was pretty unusual to hear them yelling at Alistair with *you're-in-big-trouble!* voices that reminded me of my own parents.

"Just a minute!" Alistair yelled back.

But Alistair's parents didn't wait just a minute; they both barged right into the bath-room.

"Awistair catch Haggie!" Iggy announced, proudly pointing at Alistair's toilet-fishing invention.

Alistair's parents did not look at all happy to see the three of us fishing in the toilet. They just stood there with their hands on their hips, glaring at us.

"Alistair! Stop this immediately!" Alistair's dad yelled.

"But, Dad!" Alistair protested. "I have to rescue Shirley—"

But just then something terrible happened.

The fishing line broke and disappeared down the toilet!

Shirley looked into the underwater video camera with her not-cute face and then swam away, disappearing into the murky water of the sewer.

Alistair let out a deep sigh. "I hope you're happy," he said, "because now she's probably gone for good."

BLARONITES DON'T HAVE PETS!

ALISTAIR'S MOM AND DAD led Alistair, Iggy, and me to the living room and told us to sit on the couch. I could tell they were getting ready to give us a big lecture about what we did wrong.

"Boys," Alistair's dad began, "fishing is an Earth pastime commonly done near a pond, lake, stream, river, or ocean. It is *never* done in the toilet or the city sewer system."

"I go potty fishing ONE time," Iggy declared, pointing a finger in the air.

"Shush, Iggy!" I hissed.

"We already *know* you aren't supposed to go fishing in the sewer, Dad," Alistair said.

"And we weren't just fooling around for no good reason," I added, trying to defend Alistair. "We were actually trying to rescue Alistair's pet hagfish after it accidentally got flushed down the toilet."

Alistair's parents just looked at each other and shook their heads.

"Look, this wasn't really Alistair's fault!" I insisted, wondering why Alistair was making faces at me and shaking his head *no!* as I spoke. "*Iggy's* the one who flushed Shirley down the toilet!"

"Hey!" Iggy pointed at me. "Dat not nice!"

Alistair jabbed me hard with his elbow.

I gave Alistair a *what-was-that-for?!* jab right back.

"Boys, I think we understand what happened here," said Alistair's mom. "And, Alistair, we realize this happened because you want to act like an ordinary human while you're spending time with your Earth friends."

I thought this was a weird thing to say because Alistair almost *never* behaves like an "ordinary human." I mean, if you met him you might not realize he's an *alien* from another planet, but he's definitely not in the "ordinary" category.

"However," Alistair's dad said, "lying is *not* a human characteristic you will adopt under any circumstances, Alistair. We Blaronites do not tell lies."

What lying? I wondered. *Alistair doesn't tell lies!*

"Pinocchio have a nose dat growd-ed pecuz he lying," Iggy said, pointing at his nose.

"Alistair," Alistair's dad continued, "your mother and I told you to return that hagfish to the ocean where you found it. Now we find out that you actually kept the hagfish hidden in your bedroom, and then you flushed it down the toilet."

I stared at Alistair. *So Alistair actually lied to his parents about keeping the hagfish! No wonder he didn't want to get hagfish slime all over the carpet in his room!*

Alistair just stared at the floor, looking ashamed. "*Iggy's* the one who flushed it," he mumbled.

"It doesn't matter *who* flushed the hagfish, Alistair," said Alistair's dad. "The point is that the hagfish *wouldn't* have gone down the toilet at all if you had put it back in the ocean where you found it instead of keeping it."

Secretly, I had to admit that Alistair's dad sort of had a point, but I figured Alistair would feel pretty annoyed if I started taking his dad's side right at that moment.

"You also broke an important rule of our Blaronite mission," Alistair's mom added. "Remember, Alistair, you only have permission to catch and study life-forms that are directly relevant to growing *frackenpoy*. We promised to leave everything on Earth *just the way we found it.*"

Could've fooled me, I thought, looking at Iggy and thinking about how much *he* had changed ever since Alistair's family moved into the house next door.

"*Everyone* on Earth has pets!" Alistair complained. "Why can't I have a pet?"

"I have one furry bug in a jar," Iggy offered. He was talking about his so-called pet named "Callie the caterpillar," who has probably been dead for several days. Iggy keeps telling us that Callie is "napping."

"Alistair," said Alistair's dad, "you may *look* like a human right now, but you *aren't* actually a human. Furthermore, you *will never be a human.*"

"What does that have to do with having a pet?" Alistair argued.

Alistair's dad turned red. "Because Blaronites *don't have pets*, Alistair, and that's final!"

Alistair's neck looked blotchy again. He clenched his fists, but didn't say anything for a minute.

"Of *course* nobody has pets back on Planet Blaron!" Alistair finally snapped. "Back on the home planet, the only life-forms are Blaronites and broccoli! It's *impossible* to have pets on Planet Blaron because *there aren't any animals*! And since the Blaronites can't even keep frackenpoy alive, they'd probably kill any pet they owned!"

Alistair's parents looked shocked at that outburst. I wondered if it was the first time they had ever heard Alistair get so angry.

Alistair's dad shook a finger at Alistair. "Do not speak of our home planet that way!" he said.

"Why shouldn't I?" Alistair blurted. "The Blaronites ruin *everything!*"

Alistair's dad opened his mouth to yell something, but instead he sat down in a chair and took a deep breath, trying to calm himself.

"Alistair, the hagfish you caught belongs in the wild," said Alistair's mother.

"That hagfish's name happens to be *Shirley*," Alistair said. "And she was my *pet!*"

Iggy put a sympathetic hand on Alistair's arm. "Haggie wuv me," he said, as if that would make Alistair feel better.

Alistair just stared at Iggy for a moment. Then he did something I've *never* seen him do before: He started crying. Alistair sat there with his head in his hands and just *bawled*.

Alistair's mom looked horrified.

Alistair's dad whispered something about "human tear ducts" and "saltwater discharge."

Iggy patted Alistair and said, "Haggie

in da potty," which only made Alistair cry harder.

I felt bad for Alistair, but I had no idea how to make him feel better.

Finally, Alistair's mom and dad said that it was probably time for Iggy and me to go home.

I thought that was a good idea. Things had really gone downhill since Iggy and I first came over earlier that day.

"Bye, Alistair," I said, touching his shoulder. "Um, I'm sorry about your hagfish."

Alistair nodded, but didn't say anything.

Poor Alistair, I thought as Iggy and I left his house. As if losing his pet wasn't hard enough, now he was also in huge trouble with his parents.

I hoped Alistair would get over losing that pet hagfish soon, but somehow I knew it wasn't going to be easy for him.

·11·

CHAUNCEY AND BEANIE

OUTSIDE ALISTAIR'S HOUSE, Iggy and I ran into my "frenemy" Chauncey, who was walking a very plump, fluffy dog on a leash. Actually, the dog was just sitting in the middle of the sidewalk, but Chauncey kept pulling on its leash, trying to make it walk.

"Chauncey have a doggy!" Iggy announced.

"Don't pat him right now, Iggy," Chauncey warned. "Beanie's in a terrible mood."

"I didn't know you have a dog," I said.

"It's actually my grandma's dog," Chauncey explained. "I have to take Beanie on his walks this week because Grandma hurt her back. Right, Beanie?"

Beanie wagged his little tail at the sound of his name, but made no effort to walk.

"Come on, Beanie!" Chauncey urged. "Let's get a move on!"

Beanie wasn't about to go anywhere. He lay down on the sidewalk and panted.

"Beanie's mad at me because I don't give him treats every time he does his business like my grandma does," Chauncey explained. "Grandma spoils him, but I'm going to get him into shape!"

"But how will you get him back home to your grandma's house if he won't even move?" I asked.

Chauncey shrugged. "Your sister just ran inside to find a snack that I can use as a reward." As he spoke, Chauncey pulled a bone-shaped dog biscuit from his pocket and popped it into his own mouth. He chewed the doggy biscuit and grinned down at Beanie, who stared up at him, drooling.

"I'm serious," Chauncey said, crunching. "You should try these things sometime!"

"You're eating Beanie's dog biscuits?!" I shouldn't have been surprised. It was just like Chauncey to take a dog on a walk and then steal its snack.

"Calling these cookies 'doggy biscuits' is just a marketing gimmick," Chauncey said, pulling another doggy treat from his pocket. "The same company that makes chocolate chip cookies makes these doggy treats. Same recipe; different words on the box."

I doubted that was true, but I didn't feel like getting into a dumb argument with Chauncey about dog biscuits.

"Can I twy dose chocowite chip doggy cookies?" Iggy asked.

"Sorry, Iggy." Chauncey held up empty hands. "All gone."

"NO FAIR!" Iggy shouted.

"You think *that's* no fair?" Chauncey pointed at Beanie. "What about *him*? He gets a doggy biscuit every time he does doggy doo outside. Do *I* get a treat every time I use the bathroom?"

"Yes!" said Iggy.

"No, I *don't* get a treat, Iggy! So why should I give *Beanie* all the doggy biscuits just because he pees and poops like an *ordinary dog*?"

"Maybe because they're *doggy biscuits* and he's a dog?" I suggested.

"Listen," said Chauncey. "This dog gets dog cookies *all the time* at my grandma's house!"

Chauncey loves junk food more than anything, but his mom never lets him have any. I guessed he must be pretty desperate if he was jealous of Beanie and his dog biscuits.

The front door of my house burst open and my little sister, Dottie, ran across the lawn, shouting. "Beanie! Beanie! Beanie! I have doggy tweats for youuuuuuu!"

Beanie wagged his tail and jumped up on Dottie to lick her face.

Dottie held up a pepperoni slice for Beanie. "See, Beanie? Pepperwoni for cute doggy!"

Beanie gobbled the pepperoni.

"No fair!" Iggy protested. "I want one peppowoni for Beanie, too!"

Dottie handed a piece of pepperoni to Iggy.

Beanie snatched the pepperoni from Iggy's hand, gulped it down, and then growled at Iggy.

"Hey!" Iggy protested. "Why he growlded at

me?" Iggy reached his arm toward Beanie in an attempt to pat him, but Beanie snapped at Iggy's fingers.

"STOP DAT, YOU BAD BEANIE!" Iggy dropped down on all fours, getting into an attack position.

"Oh no you don't!" I pulled Iggy to his feet before things got out of hand. "The last thing we need right now is a dogfight between you and Beanie."

"Okay, let's move it, Beanie," Chauncey pulled on Beanie's leash, but Beanie refused to budge.

"Oh, fine!" Chauncey sighed and picked up

Beanie. "Next time we go for a walk, I should just put you in my sister's baby doll carriage, Beanie."

"Wait!" Dottie ran inside the house and returned a moment later, waving a baby blanket. "I have a doggy wanket for Beanie!"

Beanie licked Dottie's hand gratefully as she tucked the blanket around him. Chauncey just rolled his eyes.

It was time for us to go inside for dinner, and as we made our way up the front steps, I spied Alistair next door, looking out his bedroom window.

I waved to Alistair, but he didn't see me. He just watched Chauncey, who was walking down the sidewalk, carrying Beanie in his arms like a baby.

·12·

DOGGIES FOR DINNER

WHILE I HELPED my mom set the table for dinner, Iggy and Dottie pretended to be brother and sister puppies named Beanie and Haggie. They cut triangles out of paper and taped them to their hair for ears. They wore socks on their hands for paws. When Mom wasn't looking, Dottie found a pair of scissors and cut a pair of her tights in half. Then she and Iggy each stuck one of the stocking legs into the waistband of their clothes for tails.

"See, Iggy?" Dottie said. "Dese our dog tails!"

Next, Dottie used the tie from Mom's bathrobe to chain Iggy to the leg of the table, as if she were tying his leash to a parking meter on the sidewalk.

"Dis your leash, Iggy," Dottie explained.

"Ruff!" Iggy replied.

"Time for doggies to sit down for dinner!" Mom announced.

But instead of sitting at the table, Dottie grabbed two plates and put them on the floor for herself and Iggy to use as dog dishes.

Mom told Iggy and Dottie to please get off the floor and sit at the table.

Iggy and Dottie pointed at their empty "dog dishes" and howled.

"Maybe we should put the dogs outside for the night," I joked.

"Ruff!" said Dottie.

"Chairs! Now!" Mom said in her *you're-not-so-cute-anymore* voice.

Iggy and Dottie whimpered as they climbed into their chairs.

As my dad sat down at the table to join us, Iggy stuck his whole face into his bowl and began to slurp his spaghetti without using a fork. He still wore socks on his paw-hands.

"You have a fork, Iggy," said my dad. "Please use it!"

"No fork!" Iggy showed Dad his sock-hands. "Paws!"

Dad was not amused.

"What is going on with you two this evening?" Mom asked.

"If we can't *have* a dog," said Dottie, "we BE a dog!"

"You can be dogs *after* dinner," Mom said.

"Mom, can we get a puppy today?" Dottie pleaded. "PLEEEEEEASE?"

Dad began to sing in a jolly voice:

If it eats and poops, then you can bet it isn't the pet we're gonna get!

Unfortunately for me, Dad loves to make up songs, and "It Isn't the Pet We're Gonna Get!" is one of his favorites.

"Everyone having a pet!" Iggy shouted. "I WANTS A PET, TOO!"

"*Alistair* doesn't have a pet," I reminded Iggy.

"Yes, he do! Awistair have a haggie-pet!"

"No, Alistair *doesn't* have a 'haggie-pet' anymore because you flushed his haggie-pet down the toilet!"

"Iggy did what?!" Mom put down her fork.

"Iggy flushed Alistair's hagfish down the toilet," I tattled.

Iggy's lip trembled. He pointed his fork at me. "Now you making me SAD!"

Uh-oh, I thought. *Iggy might have a bug-boy attack right here at the kitchen table if I don't get him to calm down.*

"Iggy, I know you didn't *mean* to flush Alistair's hagfish," I said. "It was an accident."

"Haggie going come back!" Iggy insisted.

"Iggy," said Dad. "How many times do we have to tell you not to flush things down the toilet that don't belong there?"

Iggy's face turned red.

Uh-oh, I thought.

"And this better not be about that ridiculous poo-poo-party idea either," Dad added.

Tears welled in Iggy's eyes.

Why did Dad have to call the poo-poo party "ridiculous"? I thought. Now Iggy will definitely have a meltdown!

Iggy snatched a wooden spoon from the salad bowl and chomped on it.

I once watched Iggy chew the leg off a wooden chair with "termite teeth" that popped out after Dad yelled at him, so I knew I had to get him away from the dining table fast.

"Come on, Iggy," I said, jumping up from the table.

"But you haven't finished your dinner!" Mom protested.

"Back in a minute!" I yelled, grabbing Iggy by the arm and dragging him from the room. "Iggy just needs a little time-out first."

· 13 ·

THE STORY OF SNUFFY BOO-BOO

BACK IN OUR ROOM, I gave Iggy his Human Normalizer and also one of his favorite picture books called *Big Bunny Eats a Cupcake*. It's a pretty ridiculous story, but for some reason *Big Bunny* calms Iggy down almost as fast as his Human Normalizer does.

"I hate Awistair!" Iggy blurted, without looking up from his book.

"Why do you hate Alistair?" I asked.

"Pecuz Awistair always yelling at me!"

"Alistair isn't *always* yelling at you, Iggy. He only yelled at you today because he was so angry and sad about losing his hagfish."

"Awistair and Daddy *bofe MEAN* to me," Iggy insisted.

"Listen, Iggy. Remember that time you lost Snuffy Boo-Boo?"

I reminded Iggy about the time when he and Dottie got into a huge fight in the back of our minivan.

Dottie picked up Iggy's favorite stuffed animal and threw it at Iggy.

But instead of hitting Iggy, Snuffy Boo-Boo went right out the car window and disappeared in the weeds at the side of the road!

Dad stopped the car, and we all climbed out to search for Snuffy Boo-Boo. . . .

But it was no use. It seemed that Snuffy Boo-Boo was gone for good.

"Remember how you yelled at Dottie?" I reminded Iggy.

Iggy nodded. "I sad when I lose my Snuffy."

"Well, that's exactly how Alistair feels about losing his pet hagfish."

"But Snuffy Boo-Boo come back." Iggy pointed to the beat-up stuffed frog lying on his bed, and I realized he had a point. By some weird stroke of luck, Snuffy Boo-Boo actually *did* come back.

"That's true, Iggy," I said. "You were lucky that a dog happened to find Snuffy."

I remembered the day at the park when Iggy happened to spot a dog who was chewing on something that looked like a bunch of green rags.

As it turned out, Iggy was right: the green rags actually were Iggy's very soggy and partially eaten Snuffy Boo-Boo.

"But, Iggy," I continued, "remember how Dottie tried to make you feel better *before* you got Snuffy back?"

TA-DA! SEE, IGGY? I GIVING YOU MY TOYS!

I reminded Iggy how Dottie drew about twenty pictures of Snuffy Boo-Boo for him, and how she covered Iggy's bed with a mountain of her own toys.

Iggy listened and nodded. "Dano," he said, pointing a finger in the air, "you giving me a gweat idea!"

"What is it?"

Iggy found some paper and a box of crayons. "I going *make a pwesent* for Awistair!" he announced.

Iggy got to work.

A few minutes later, he handed me his drawing—a picture of a hagfish waving good-bye from a toilet.

Beneath the picture, Iggy attempted to write the words, "Good-bye, Haggie! I'm sorry. Love, Iggy."

Compared to most of Iggy's scribbly drawings, this drawing was actually pretty good.

"I'm sure Alistair will like your picture, Iggy," I said, thinking that Alistair would at least appreciate an apology.

"No," Iggy said. "Awistair going to WUV dis picture! When he seeing dis picture I make-ted for him, he won't feel sad for his Haggie."

I looked at Iggy and thought how much he had to learn about people. I mean, even an alien from Planet Blaron is going to miss his lost pet for more than one day.

CALLIE AND MISS DAISY

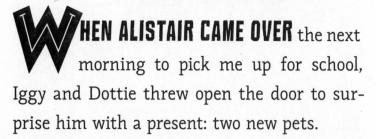

WHEN ALISTAIR CAME OVER the next morning to pick me up for school, Iggy and Dottie threw open the door to surprise him with a present: two new pets.

"TA-DA!" Iggy and Dottie shouted. "NEW PETS FOR YOU!"

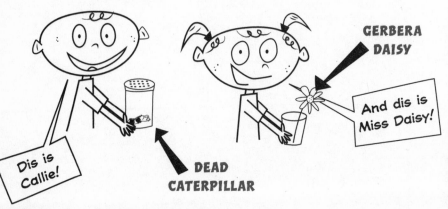

Dis is Callie!

DEAD CATERPILLAR

GERBERA DAISY

And dis is Miss Daisy!

"See, Awistair?" Iggy said. "Callie never going wun away fwum you!!"

"Interesting." Alistair looked at the pink flower in a pot and the motionless caterpillar in the jar. "What you have here is a *Malacosoma americanum (mors)* and a *Gerbera jamesonii*," he said.

It's just like Alistair to know the Latin names for a caterpillar and a daisy, I thought.

Iggy shook his head. "No," he said. "Dis *not* a 'mawacocofum'; dis a *caterpiddar*."

I nudged Iggy. "Remember what you wanted to tell Alistair?"

"I sorry I flushted Haggie in da potty," Iggy said, just like he had practiced.

"I know you're sorry, Iggy."

Alistair's eyes looked red and puffy, and I guessed he had been crying about losing Shirley.

"Callie can make you happy," Iggy suggested.

Alistair just stared at Iggy. "That's nice of

you to share your dead caterpillar with me, Iggy."

Iggy tapped on the glass jar. "Callie *napping*."

"But even if I took this deceased caterpillar home with me," Alistair continued, "I would still miss Shirley, and you and Dottie would miss Callie and Miss Daisy. Think about it: There would be three sad people instead of just one."

Iggy thought about it. "Maybe *four* sad peoples becuz my caterpiddar also feeling sad."

"Time to go to school everyone!" Mom grabbed her purse and keys and basically bulldozed all of us out the front door.

Mom, Iggy, and Dottie climbed into our minivan while Alistair and I walked down the sidewalk in the opposite direction.

We didn't say much as we made our way to school, but every now and then, Alistair paused and peered down into a storm drain opening with his flashlight.

I didn't want to hurt Alistair's feelings, but if you ask me, it seemed pretty unlikely that Shirley was still alive down there.

"Alistair," I said, "do you really think a hagfish could survive getting flushed?"

"I was just researching that question last night," Alistair said, "and I read about live alligators and snakes being discovered in the sewers. There was also a story about someone's pet goldfish who survived getting flushed."

"That's good news," I said.

Alistair sighed. "On the other hand, Shirley might be gone for good."

"But there's always a reason to hope," I said. I didn't really believe it, but when I saw how sad Alistair looked, I couldn't help trying to make him feel a little better.

PET SADNESS

AT SCHOOL, Alistair had a tough time concentrating. Usually this isn't a problem for him because Alistair is so smart, he doesn't even need to listen to Mr. Binns in order to understand our assignments. He usually finishes his worksheets in about half a minute and then he spends his time drawing diagrams for new robots or nibbling on broccoli florets that he brings in little snack bags.

But today was different. Today, Alistair

just sat at our worktable, staring at nothing.

It really bugged me that Alistair was acting so spacey because the two of us had signed up to work on a science presentation together, and to be honest, I had kind of been counting on Alistair to come up with a smart idea and then do most of the work.

I glanced at Alistair's notebook and saw that it was covered with drawings of Shirley. He had also written a sad letter to her:

Dear Shirley,
I miss you so much. I feel like you're still close by even though you're so far away. I'm sorry I didn't value our time together more. Each moment was precious. I will never, ever forget you, Shirley, my one-and-only, my pet!

"Come on, Alistair," I said. "We're supposed to be working on our science presentation."

Alistair shook his head. "I'm too distraught to work on the presentation."

"What's that supposed to mean?" I asked.

Alistair looked at me. "Don't you remember? We were planning to do our presentation on the topic of *hagfish*! I'm feeling pretty upset right now."

"Oh," I said. "I forgot."

"And as you know," Alistair continued, "we no longer *have* a hagfish."

"So we'll change our topic," I suggested.

"That isn't possible," Alistair said, "because there's nothing I'm curious about right now."

"Of course there is!" I said, now even more worried that I was going to get stuck doing the whole project on my own. "You're always curious about stuff!"

Alistair shook his head. "Something has changed," he said.

"What do you mean?"

"I feel like something inside me hurts, but it's not a body part. All I know is that I don't want to do anything except think about Shirley."

"That's probably normal," I said. "I mean, you're still really sad."

"It's worse than 'sad.'"

"I mean, you really *miss* Shirley a lot. You've lost something. So it's normal that you feel down. Right?"

Alistair thought for a moment. "Maybe I feel a new emotion called *'pet sad.'*"

"Then the best thing to do is to just get your mind off Shirley and try to think about something else for a while," I suggested. "What about that slime-mold stuff you were telling me about a few days ago? Remember how excited you were when you found a real slime mold in your own yard? I bet *that* would make a great topic!"

Alistair shrugged. "I *used* to think slime mold was interesting."

"And it is interesting! Slime mold would make a *great* topic for our presentation!"

To be honest, I wasn't really sure if slime mold would be a great topic, but we had a lot of work to get done, and Alistair really needed to get started.

"The problem," Alistair said, "is that I don't *care* about slime mold like I care about Shirley."

"Of course you don't," I said. "Who would? But that doesn't mean we can't do a perfectly okay B-plus presentation on slime mold."

Alistair sighed. "I guess you're right," he said.

"Of course I'm right."

Alistair picked up his pencil. I was happy to see him finally start writing a few notes about slime mold.

But just my luck: right when Alistair was finally starting to work on our science presentation, Chauncey snuck up behind us and swiped Alistair's notebook!

Alistair and I turned to see Chauncey smirking as he read Alistair's private letter to Shirley.

"WHO'S SHIRLEY?" Chauncey blabbed.

"Mind your own beeswax, Chauncey!" I tried to grab Alistair's notebook, but Chauncey was too quick for me. He held the notebook over my head with his long, ape-like arms.

"Hey, everybody!" Chauncey announced. "ALISTAIR HAS A GIRLFRIEND!"

Everyone in the class turned to stare at Alistair.

"'Dear Shirley'" Chauncey read, faking an accent that was supposed to sound French but

instead just sounded annoying: "'I mees you zoooooo much! I feel like you are steel cloze by! Even zoe you are far away!'"

Alistair looked like a deer caught in the headlights of an oncoming car as Chauncey read his "Dear Shirley" letter aloud to the whole class.

"Sounds like a long-distance relationship, Alistair," Chauncey teased.

"Well, it's not really—" Alistair began, but Chauncey cut him off and kept reading:

"'I vill never ever forget you! SHIRLEY! MA DAHLING! MA PET!'"

"I'll take that, thank you very much!"

Mr. Binns came up behind Chauncey and snatched the notebook away from him. "Back to your seat, Chauncey."

Mr. Binns clapped his hands to make everyone in the classroom stop giggling. "I apologize for Chauncey's behavior, Alistair," he said, handing the Shirley-covered notebook back to Alistair.

"Listen, people," Mr. Binns continued. "There is no place for rude behavior like what Chauncey just did in this classroom. Understand?"

Everyone got quiet. Chauncey scowled.

"Furthermore, I don't want any boy in this class to ever feel bad just because he likes a girl. That is Alistair's personal business."

That got everyone giggling again. *Didn't Mr. Binns know when to stop?*

"Mr. Binns?" I raised my hand, feeling that I should at least try to help Alistair with this situation.

"Yes, Daniel?"

"I just want to say that Shirley isn't actually Alistair's girlfriend." I figured that if I didn't speak up for Alistair, the teasing would never end. "Shirley was Alistair's *pet,* and he's sad because he lost her yesterday."

Hearing that news, everyone stopped giggling. In Mr. Binns's classroom, losing a girlfriend or boyfriend is a big joke, but losing a pet is serious business.

"We had to put my dog, Lady, to sleep last summer because she was really sick," a girl named Catherine said. "I cried for a whole week. Even my dad cried."

"One of my pet frogs died just a couple weeks ago," a boy named Carlos said.

It turned out that just about everyone in Mr. Binns's classroom except Chauncey had either lost a pet or knew someone who did.

"Pets are very important to us," Mr. Binns said, after everyone shared a story. "So we can all understand how Alistair must feel right now. Right, Chauncey?"

Chauncey shrugged. "All pets do is beg for snacks," he said.

"No they don't!" said Catherine. "Lady could do lots of tricks! She could even ride a scooter!"

Everyone wanted to hear more about Catherine's dog Lady and the scooter, but Mr. Binns interrupted, saying that Chauncey needed to apologize to Alistair right now.

Chauncey fidgeted but finally mumbled a not-very-sincere "*Sorry.*"

"It's okay, Chauncey," Alistair said. "I'm actually *glad* you read my letter to the class."

Mr. Binns and Chauncey looked surprised.

"Why are you glad, Alistair?" Mr. Binns asked.

"Because I had no idea that so many people in this class have also gone through this terrible pet sadness I'm feeling." Alistair looked around the room. "And if you all survived it, then maybe I will, too."

Everyone, including Mr. Binns, just stared at Alistair. Alistair doesn't talk in class very often, and I think nobody really knows what to expect from him.

Finally, Mr. Binns just said, "It's hard to lose a pet, Alistair. We all hope you feel better soon."

Then Mr. Binns started talking about our science projects, and the day went on as usual.

But one thing was different: now that everyone in our class knew that Alistair had lost his pet, they started doing little things to make him feel better. By the end of the school day, Alistair's desk was covered with notes and cards—pictures of dogs, cats, fish, and reptiles from the kids in our class. Alistair hadn't told the class what type of pet he lost, so people just drew whatever animal they liked best.

"I feel a little better," Alistair admitted as we walked home from school at the end of the day. "It's strange how it helps, just knowing that so many children have also lost their pets. . . ."

Alistair's voice trailed off. He paused and stepped off the sidewalk and knelt next to a storm drain. "SHIRLEY?" he called, yelling down into the gutter. "SHIIIIRLEEEEY!"

I started yelling too: "SHIRRRRRRLEEEEEEY!"

After a few minutes, we both got tired of yelling.

"Let's go, Alistair," I said. "After I drop off my stuff at home, I'll come over so we can work on our slime-mold project, okay?"

"Okay." Alistair sighed.

"And once we finish the project we could go back to my house to build some Technoblok models."

"I guess so," Alistair said. "Sure."

I knew Alistair didn't really want to work on the slime-mold project or even build Technobloks. I knew he only wanted to do one thing—get Shirley back.

THE MYSTERY MONSTER

IT WAS MY DAD'S work-from-home day, and when I got home, I found him lying on the couch in front of the television, napping on top of a huge pile of clean laundry. He looked pretty ridiculous because Iggy and Dottie had clipped a bunch of Dottie's plastic barrettes in his hair, which stuck up in little pigtails all over his head. He was also covered with lots of little pants, T-shirts, and underwear that Iggy and Dottie had placed on top of him like tiny baby blankets.

Iggy and Dottie sat under the dining table, playing a game they call Angry Kitty, which basically means that Iggy pretends to be Dottie's grouchy pet cat.

"Time to brush your fur, Kitty!" Dottie announced, holding a hairbrush.

"MEOW! MEOW! HISSSSSSS!" Iggy hissed and pretended to scratch Dottie with his cat claws.

"No, Angwy Kitty!" Dottie shook a finger at Iggy. "You need your booful fur-style! And den you need your bubble baf and your nap and go potty in your litter box!"

Dottie pointed at Iggy's pretend "litter box," which was actually a bunch of pages from our local newspaper, *The Daily Journal,* placed on the floor next to some cereal bowls that were supposed to be Angry Kitty's cat-food dishes.

I was just about to wake up Dad to make fun of his hairstyle when something in the newspaper caught Iggy's attention: "Hey!" Iggy shouted. "Dat monster look like Haggie!"

"Dat a gwoss monster," Dottie commented.

I figured the two of them were just playing around, but I was curious so I walked over to Iggy and Dottie to take a look.

"See?" Iggy said, pointing at the newspaper. "Dat Haggie!"

There in the newspaper was a black-and-white photo of a strange creature that looked like some kind of small sea monster.

I can't believe it! I thought. *Iggy is right!*

There, in the newspaper, was a photograph of Alistair's pet hagfish!

THE DAILY JOURNAL

SEA MONSTER OF THE SEWER?

Local Sewer Worker Gets a Nasty Suprise on the Job!

Duane Ponders got a strange surprise when he climbed into a manhole to carry out a routine inspection yesterday.

The local sewer worker "heard something go 'splash!' in the water" and climbed down his ladder to take a look at what he thought was probably a rat.

What Ponders saw swimming in the sewer was no rat.

"I don't know if it was some kind of monster, or an alien, or what," Ponders told *The Daily Journal*, "but I've never seen anything like it before in my life!"

to get out of the sewer.

"When my buddies saw me come out of that manhole, they thought I had seen a ghost," Ponders said. "I told them, 'I don't believe in ghosts, but now I might believe in sewer monsters!'"

The situation is being investigated and residents are encouraged to report anything unusual.

Although terrified, Ponders managed to pull out his camera and snap a picture of the "monster" before hurrying back up the ladder

If this is really a photograph of Shirley, it means that she survived getting flushed and that she's probably still swimming around down in the sewer, I thought.

I tore the news article from the paper and jumped to my feet. I knew I had to tell Alistair right away.

THE EXPERIMENT

"HEY, ALISTAIR!" I yelled, waving the newspaper article in my hand as I ran across my front yard into Alistair's yard. "You have to read this news article!"

Alistair stood still as a statue in his front yard, staring down at something in the grass.

"Look, Daniel," Alistair said, pointing down at a yellow-green, slimy blob. "This is a *Fuligo septica*, also commonly known by the name dog-vomit slime mold."

I once saw a dog barf up some grass when I was at the park, and that's pretty much what the slime mold looked like. "Cool!" I told Alistair, wanting him to know I was impressed. "But you really have to read this news article *right now*!"

Alistair finally looked at the newspaper I was waving under his nose, and when he saw the photograph of a hagfish, a huge smile spread across his face.

"It's her!" Alistair looked up at me and then back down at the newspaper. "This means she's still alive down there!"

"I know!' I said. "Isn't this great news?"

"Yes, but it means we have to find a way

to get her out of there!" Alistair turned and began to pace back and forth.

"If your parents would just give you back your watch, it would be a lot easier to solve this problem," I complained. To be honest, I also really missed playing with the amazing flying robots Alistair and I used to make with his alien technology.

Alistair plucked a broccoli floret from one of the plants growing in clay pots near his front porch. "Those sewer pipes are like a huge underground maze beneath the city," he said, pausing to nibble a piece of broccoli. "And that means that a lost hagfish could be just about anywhere."

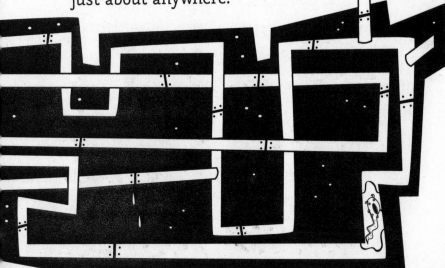

But before Alistair and I could figure out how to rescue Shirley, Iggy and Dottie came running toward us.

"HEY, AWISTAIR!" Iggy shouted. "DADDY SAY WE CAN PLAY OUTSIDE WIF YOU AND DANO NOW!"

"Stop!" Alistair warned, pointing at the ground. "Watch out for the slime mold!"

"YUCK!" Iggy shouted when he saw what Alistair was pointing toward. "DOTTIE, LOOK AT DESE GWASS BOOGERS!"

"It's called *slime mold*, Iggy," Alistair said. "It's actually one big amoeba—a blob of protoplasm."

"What dis poodopassum doos?" Iggy asked.

"It can do a lot!"

Alistair told Iggy and Dottie all about slime mold. "For example," Alistair said, "even though it doesn't have legs or feet, a dog-vomit slime mold can *move*. It can stretch itself toward food or even crawl *very slowly* across the ground."

"And here's something really amazing: a slime mold doesn't have a brain, but it can actually solve problems," Alistair continued.

"Like math problems?" I asked, suddenly curious. (I had to admit this slime-mold stuff was a lot weirder—and more interesting— than I had expected!)

One plus one equals two! Seven plus nine equals three! Fifty plus eleventy equals four!

"It can't solve *math problems*," Alistair said, giving me a *why-are-humans-so-dumb?* look. "But I read about an experiment where a slime mold found its way through a maze to reach a cookie."

"Good boy, Slimy!" Iggy said, squatting down next to the slime mold as if it were a pet dog.

"Do you think *this* slime mold could find its way through a maze?" I asked.

"Maybe it could," Alistair said, "if it's one of the *smart* ones."

How can something that has no brain be 'smart'? I wondered. It sure didn't *look* very smart. It looked like a gooey puddle of dog puke.

"Hey," I said, "we should do the slime-mold maze experiment for our science project! I bet Mr. Binns would love it!" I was really curious to see whether the yellow-green glob on the ground could actually move on its own. In fact, I probably would have wanted to do the experiment even if it didn't count for a grade!

"First, we have to build a maze," Alistair said.

"I can do that," I said.

"And we'll need a cookie," Alistair added.

"We can get cookies for Slimy!"

While Iggy and Dottie ran back home to get cookies, Alistair and I began to build our maze. We knew we still needed to rescue Shirley, but we figured we might as well get the experiment started first since it was due the next day.

·18·

A WILD RIDE

A MINUTE LATER, Iggy and Dottie returned with cookies to use as bait for the slime mold.

We worked fast to build our slime-mold maze, and when we finished Alistair gently picked up the gloppy slime mold from the grass and placed it inside the maze.

"Next we hide the cookie in the maze," Alistair explained, placing the cookie on the opposite side of the maze, "and we'll record how long it takes our slime mold to find it."

We both stared at our slime mold, which just sat there in the maze.

"It isn't even moving," I said.

"It's going to move *very slowly*, Daniel," Alistair reminded me. "We have to be patient."

That's when Alistair and I heard loud squawking sounds overhead: "BAWK! BAWK! BAWK!"

I looked up and couldn't believe my eyes: Iggy and Dottie were flying around Alistair's yard!

Dottie was perched on Iggy's back as if she were riding a flying horse or a tiny airplane! Alistair and I stared up at them as they soared overhead. Dottie screamed like a kid on a roller coaster as Iggy swooped down low and then zoomed up high, nearly touching the tops of the oak trees in Alistair's yard.

How will we ever get Iggy and Dottie down from there? I wondered, panicking. *What if they fall? What if Iggy flies far away and gets lost?*

"The odd thing about this," Alistair observed, "is that Iggy wasn't even upset about anything this time."

With Iggy and Dottie zooming over our heads, I told Alistair how Iggy sometimes transforms when he gets really happy about something, like when he was super-excited to meet Alistair's new pet.

"This could be a problem," Alistair said, sounding more concerned.

I had a bad feeling that Alistair was right about that.

Iggy circled overhead and then swooped down low, giggling as he tried to dive-bomb us.

Instead of ducking, Alistair seized the opportunity to capture Iggy. "Now!" he hissed. "GRAB HIM!!"

We pounced: Alistair grabbed one of Iggy's legs and I grabbed the other.

Dottie screamed. Iggy kicked his feet hard, trying to shake us off. "STOP DAT!!" Iggy shouted. "LET GO!"

"LAND, IGGY!" Alistair and I yelled.

Instead of landing, Iggy zoomed straight up in the air like a rocket, with Dottie screeching and clinging to his T-shirt and Alistair and me each hanging on to one of his legs!

Now all three of us were screaming: "STOP, IGGY! STOP!!"

I glanced down and felt even queasier than I did when I made the mistake of riding The

Dizzy Devil last summer at a carnival. The Dizzy Devil is scary, but it's nothing compared to hanging on to a crazy preschooler with insect wings.

"LAND, IGGY!" all three of us shouted. *"LAND!!"*

I glimpsed our school from above as Iggy circled over the rooftops and trees of our neighborhood. Then, a few blocks away, I spotted Chauncey leaving his grandma's house to walk Beanie.

Beanie spied us zooming across the sky and started barking like crazy.

Uh-oh! I thought. *What if Chauncey sees all of us flying through the air?*

Startled by Beanie's loud yapping, Iggy made a sharp turn and flew back to the cover of trees in Alistair's yard.

A second later, we all crash-landed on Alistair's lawn, rolling and somersaulting over the grass.

Once I caught my breath, I stood up, stuck

the Human Normalizer into Iggy's mouth, and got ready to yell at Iggy like I had never yelled before.

Then something strange happened: a bright light surrounded Alistair, Iggy, Dottie, and me. My skin tingled and itched. I felt weightless: I could see my feet standing on the ground, but I couldn't move them.

A moment later, all four of us had vanished from Earth.

· 19 ·

BUNNIES IN SPACE

"OH DIS SO AWESOME!" Iggy shouted. "WE FLY TO A BERFDAY PARTY!"

Alistair, Iggy, Dottie, and I found ourselves in a room filled with colorful balloons.

Sitting across from me, Alistair looked worried. He mouthed one word: *"Bumblepod."*

I had been transported aboard the Spaceship Bumblepod before, and I remembered how the Blaronites had used images from Iggy's mind to make their alien environment look less scary to Iggy and me. This time, it looked like the Blaronites had added some details from Dottie's mind, too.

"IGGY! LOOK!" Dottie jumped up from the table and ran toward a bunch of sparkling dresses, hats, and shoes. "Dese dwesses so booful!" Dottie pulled a pink princess dress over her regular clothes and twirled around the room. She placed a glittering tiara on her head.

Iggy found a "booful dwess" decorated with a bunch of jewels and even coins. "I having dis piwate dwess!" Iggy shouted.

"No, Iggy!" Dottie snatched the "pirate-dress" away from Iggy. "Dese booful dwesses all for me!"

But before Iggy could grab the dress back from Dottie, the two of them stopped fighting and froze, staring at the two enormous rabbits that had just hopped into the room.

I think rabbits were pretty much the last thing any of us expected to see on Spaceship Bumblepod, and these bunnies were extra-

surprising since they were about the size of
horses or cows.

"Don't forget the cupcakes, Miss Bubble,"
said the first giant rabbit, who had white fur
and pink eyes.

"Whoops! Be right back!" said the second
rabbit, who had light-brown fur.

Iggy and Dottie just stared with their
mouths hanging open. Then they turned to
each other and screamed the title of their
favorite book: *"BIG BUNNY EATS A CUPCAKE!!"*

Now it made sense: The Blaronites must
have used Iggy's and Dottie's memory of their
favorite *Big Bunny Eats a Cupcake* book to
disguise themselves! And maybe the rabbits

in Iggy's and Dottie's imaginations look way bigger than ordinary bunnies.

"Welcome to the Spaceship Bumblepod, Iggy, Dottie, Daniel, and Alistair," said the first giant rabbit. "My name is Commander Stickyfoot, Senior Commander of the Bumblepod, and this is my colleague, Miss Bubbles."

"YOUR NAMES IS BIG BUNNY!" Iggy and Dottie shouted, pointing at the two giant rabbits.

You would think that a giant bunny would be really cute and cuddly, but if you ask me, Commander Stickyfoot was a little *scary*. For one thing, those rodent teeth of his looked dangerous.

"Now," said Commander Stickyfoot, "while Miss Bubbles takes Iggy and Dottie to the Big Bunny Birthday Party, Alistair and Daniel will stay here with me to discuss an important matter."

Iggy and Dottie jumped up and down

and chanted, "BIG BUNNY BERFDAY! BIG BUNNY BERFDAY!" as they followed Miss Bubbles to some other part of the spaceship.

"Am I in trouble?" Alistair asked.

Commander Stickyfoot didn't answer right away because he was trying to fit his rabbit body into a human-sized chair at the table, while also holding a cupcake in his front paws. Finally, Commander Stickyfoot gave up and decided to sit on the floor, like an ordinary rabbit.

"Now, Alistair," said Commander Stickyfoot, in between nibbles of his cupcake, "what makes you think you're in trouble?"

"I'm thinking it's the only reason you would transport me to Spaceship Bumblepod without any warning, isn't it?"

"Well, we *might* bring you here to honor you with a prize for something you did well!" said Commander Stickyfoot.

Alistair looked hopeful.

"But a reward is *not* why you're here today."

Alistair sighed.

"Alistair," said Commander Stickyfoot, "we've noticed a couple problems. Number one: you're allowing Iggy to fly around the neighborhood. Number two: you lost a hagfish in the sewer."

"Yes, but—"

Commander Stickyfoot raised a paw to silence Alistair.

"Alistair, you *must* get that hagfish out of the sewer or your mission is over. Understand?"

Alistair looked pale. "I understand."

"And if we hear about any more problems, it's back to Planet Blaron for you!"

When I heard that, I couldn't keep quiet anymore. "Just a minute, Commander Stickyfoot!" I interrupted. "If Alistair gets sent back to Planet Blaron, where would that leave me and Iggy?"

"That would leave you both on planet Earth, of course," said Commander Stickyfoot, totally missing my point.

"But I couldn't deal with Iggy all by myself, without Alistair's help!" I protested.

Commander Stickyfoot hopped to the other side of the table, leaving a small pile of round rabbit poops behind. He picked up another broccoli cupcake.

"Daniel," Commander Stickyfoot said, between nibbles of his cupcake, "it seems that you have more problems when you're *with* Alistair than when you're on your own."

"That's not true," I argued.

Commander Stickyfoot stared at me with his pink rabbit eyes. "If Alistair hadn't given Iggy his hagfish to hold, it wouldn't have ended up falling into the swimming pool in the first place."

"She fell into a *toilet!*" Alistair blurted, suddenly finding his voice again. "Not a swimming pool!"

"Swimming pool, toilet . . . same difference," said Commander Stickyfoot.

"It isn't the same at all!" Alistair practically yelled.

"But Commander Stickyfoot," I said, trying to keep calm since Alistair looked like he was about to blow a fuse, "the bottom line is that even if a few mistakes happen, it's *really important* for Alistair to stay right where he is, on planet Earth."

"And why is that, Daniel?" Commander Stickyfoot asked.

I imagined my life without Alistair. There would be nobody to build awesome Technoblok models with and nobody to complain to about Iggy when he's bugging me. I knew why he had to stay on Earth: *Because if Alistair got sent back to Planet Blaron, I would miss my best friend way too much.*

· 20 ·

THE DANGEROUS PLAN

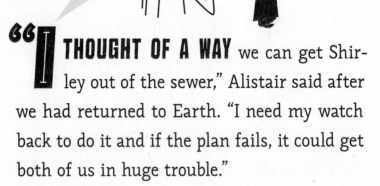

"I THOUGHT OF A WAY we can get Shirley out of the sewer," Alistair said after we had returned to Earth. "I need my watch back to do it and if the plan fails, it could get both of us in huge trouble."

"I don't care," I said. "Let's try it." I knew I had to help Alistair get Shirley back no matter what.

Alistair lowered his voice and leaned close to me. "My parents keep my watch locked in a safe in their bedroom. Every night, my mom and dad take off their own watches and lock them up for the night in the same safe. So here's my plan: tonight I'll spy on my parents and memorize the pass code to the safe. Then, when my parents are asleep, we'll sneak into their room to steal my watch out of the safe and program it to rescue Shirley!"

I knew it was wrong of us to sneak Alistair's watch from the safe where his parents were hiding it. On the other hand, the plan sounded pretty exciting.

"There's just one problem," Alistair said.

"What's that?"

"When we first moved to Earth, Dad trained himself to sleep with one of his eyes open."

"How can he sleep with one eye open?" I asked.

"Well, most of my dad's brain is sleeping, but his 'guard eyeball' stays awake in case of an intruder. It's sort of like a burglar alarm."

"Alistair," I said, "I don't see how we'll be able to sneak the watch from your dad's room if he sleeps with one eye open."

Alistair thought for a moment. "Unless Iggy could help us by creating a distraction."

I pictured Iggy getting excited about something and waking up both of Alistair's parents. "I doubt Iggy would be much help," I said.

"But I'm not talking about *human* Iggy," Alistair explained. "I'm talking about *flying-insect* Iggy. And I have a theory that Dottie knows how to make our bug boy fly."

THE SECRET TICKLE

"DOTTIE," ALISTAIR SAID, "how do you make Iggy grow wings?"

Alistair was determined to figure out the secret to making Iggy sprout wings on command, since we might need "flying Iggy" to help distract Alistair's dad.

"My dad won't wake up if his 'guard-eyeball' thinks it's just an insect flying around his room," Alistair explained. "Iggy's job is to keep my dad distracted while I sneak my watch out of the safe." Then he turned to Dottie.

If you wants Iggy to fly," Dottie said, "you has to tickle on his belly button."

I caught Alistair's eye. *Was it really that simple?*

"Like dis way." Dottie lifted Iggy's shirt and tickled his belly button with her little finger. "Fly, Iggy, fly!"

Iggy burst into giggles as wings sprouted from his shoulder blades.

Alistair and I were amazed.

So it's true! I thought. *Dottie really does know how to control Iggy's bug traits!!*

Dottie told us how to make Iggy grow a stinger; how Iggy can "spin one spiderweb from his bottom"; how to make Iggy grow "sticky, walk-on-the-ceiling toes"; and how to make "booful budderfly wings" sprout from Iggy's back.

"This means our plan is a 'go,'" Alistair whispered as Dottie kept chatting about how to trigger Iggy's bug traits. "Tonight Iggy will help us steal the watch!"

·22·

THE NIGHTTIME ADVENTURE

IT'S LUCKY my mom and dad don't believe half the stuff Iggy tells them because instead of eating dinner, he ended up blabbing our secret plan "to sneak to Awistair's house in da nighttime."

I gave Iggy his Human Normalizer while Dottie gave him one of her "kitty-cat head scratchies."

Finally, Iggy got calm enough to let me roll him into his bed. He seemed to fall asleep the moment his head hit the pillow.

Once Iggy fell sleep, Dottie went back to
her room and I climbed up to the top bunk.

After that, I must have dozed off because
the next thing I heard was the crackly sound
of Alistair's voice coming through my walkie-
talkie:

I climbed down the ladder from my bed, grabbed my jacket and a flashlight, and put on my shoes. When I was ready, I gave Iggy a little shake to wake him up. "Iggy!" I whispered, "Wake up!"

I had expected Iggy to bounce right out of bed since he had been so excited about our plan. Instead of waking up, Iggy grabbed my hand and tried to stick my thumb in his mouth like a pacifier.

"Iggy!" I pulled my thumb out of his mouth. "Wake up!"

Iggy dove under the blankets.

I pulled the blankets off Iggy and tried to stuff his uncooperative feet into shoes.

"Iggy," I said, "it's time for our adventure at Alistair's house!"

"I tired," Iggy said.

"Why Iggy still sweeping?" Dottie peered into our room, all dressed and ready to go.

"Dottie, maybe you can wake up Iggy," I suggested.

"Come on, Kitty," Dottie cooed, tickling Iggy under his chin. "Let's go get some cat tweats!"

Luckily, Dottie's cat game worked! A minute later, the three of us tiptoed through the darkness toward Alistair's house.

23

A RUDE AWAKENING

BUT WHEN WE GOT TO Alistair's house, Iggy headed straight for Alistair's couch and curled up for a nap.

"Iggy want to sweep," Dottie explained.

"We just need your help for a few minutes, Iggy," Alistair said. "Then you can go back to bed, okay?"

"Mmph," Iggy mumbled from the couch.

"My parents are asleep in that room down the hall," Alistair explained, pointing to a closed door at the end of the hallway. "Iggy, your job is to fly around and distract my dad while I get my watch, okay?"

"Smooboof," Iggy mumbled.

"Daniel, you and Dottie will stand guard right here in the hallway."

"Okay."

"I should also warn you that my parents *take off their human disguises* when they go to bed at night," Alistair added. "Just remember that the people in that room might look weird but they aren't monsters.

"Okay, Awistair," Dottie said.

To be honest, I felt a little queasy at the idea of seeing Alistair's mom and dad without their human disguises.

"Okay, Dottie," Alistair said. "Time to activate Iggy's wings!"

Dottie tickled Iggy's tummy, but this time he didn't giggle. "Stop dat, Dottie!" Iggy grumbled.

"Come on, little butterfly," Dottie coaxed. "Wake up and fly!"

"STOP DAT!" Iggy yelled. Instead of butterfly wings, Iggy's wasp wings and several
stingers popped out.

Now Iggy was completely awake, but instead of helping us, he was buzzing around
the room, knocking books, scientific tools,
and potted broccoli plants to the floor.

"Iggy!" Alistair whispered, "we have to do
this quickly!" Alistair's hand rested on the
doorknob to his parents' room. "When I open
this door, you need to distract my dad by flying around until you see me take the watch
out of the safe. Understand?"

Iggy didn't answer; he just kept buzzing around the room.

Alistair frowned at Iggy, but decided he'd better go ahead and try to get the watch. He opened the door to his parents' room. Without hesitating, Iggy zoomed right through it toward Alistair's mom and dad.

24

THE WATCHFUL EYE

IF YOU COULD REMOVE the entire surface of your body from your hair to your toes the way a scuba diver peels off a wet suit and then hang it over a chair, you might see something like what we saw in Alistair's parents' room.

Seeing those limp "human body disguises" hanging over a chair was freaky enough. I tried not to look up where both of Alistair's parents were asleep with their baggy bodies stuck to the ceiling and their eyeball stalks all tangled together.

Now I see why Alistair thinks his pet hagfish is "cute," I thought. *Compared to Alistair's parents without their disguises, Shirley could probably win a beauty contest.*

"That floating ball over there is the safe," Alistair whispered, pointing to a transparent ball that floated next to the human disguises. "It's protected by a force field."

I had pictured something a lot sturdier, like a big metal box with a heavy padlock. This thing looked like a transparent bubble with three watches floating inside it—one for each member of Alistair's family.

The weirdest part of the whole scene was Alistair's dad's single open eye—a giant eyeball that turned in circles and blinked slowly as it tracked Iggy's insect movements while Alistair tapped the safe's complicated pass code.

The plan actually seemed to be working until Alistair's dad's eyeball suddenly moved too close to Iggy.

Instead of flying away, Iggy stung the eyeball with his wasp stinger.

"No, Iggy!" Dottie yelled. "Dat eyeball monster is Awistair's dad!

Now Alistair's dad will wake up and kill us, I thought.

But instead of waking up Alistair's dad, the "security guard" eyeball decided to kill Iggy on its own.

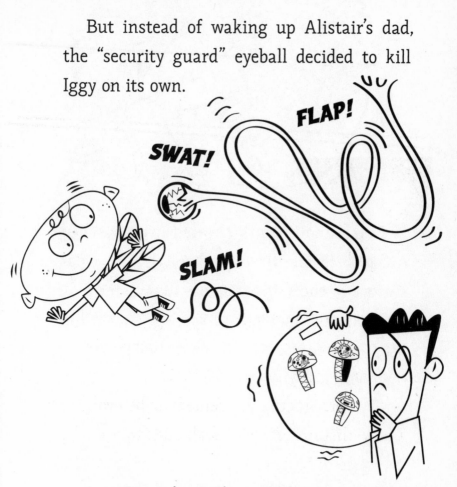

As Alistair's dad's eyeball chased Iggy, swatting at him as he zipped around the room, Alistair kept typing out what had to be the longest pass code in the universe.

Finally, Alistair managed to open the safe's force field.

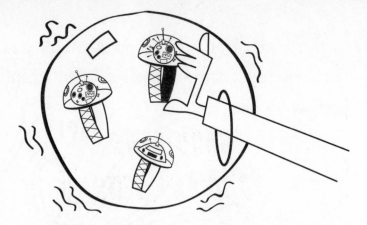

Dottie and I silently cheered as we watched Alistair reach directly through the clear surface of the safe to remove his watch!

Without a moment to spare, Alistair and Iggy hurried from the room and slammed the door behind them.

25

GOOD NEWS
AND BAD NEWS

ONCE IGGY AND DOTTIE were back home and tucked into their beds, Alistair and I went outside with our flashlights and Alistair's watch. We also brought a weird-looking robot that Alistair had built very quickly using a bunch of Technobloks and bath toys. It looked like a mermaid with crab claws and a motor.

We took our robot to a storm-drain opening at the edge of the sidewalk and Alistair popped open the clear dome that covers his watch.

Inside the watch, tiny, multicolored bubbles moved back and forth. "That's odd."
Alistair frowned as he quickly tapped out
a complicated pattern.

"What's odd?"

Alistair looked worried. "We may have a
problem here."

A small screen on his watch displayed
a message in the Blaronite language. Alistair
translated it as he read aloud:

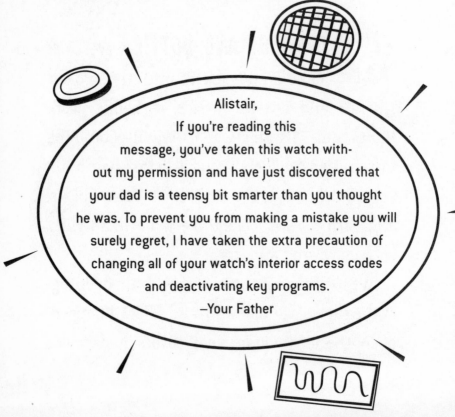

Alistair,
If you're reading this
message, you've taken this watch without my permission and have just discovered that
your dad is a teensy bit smarter than you thought
he was. To prevent you from making a mistake you will
surely regret, I have taken the extra precaution of
changing all of your watch's interior access codes
and deactivating key programs.
—Your Father

Alistair was so mad, I could practically see smoke coming out of his ears. "I can't believe Dad changed all the pass codes on my watch!" Alistair plunked himself down on the curb. "Now I'll end up getting sent back to Planet Blaron just because Dad won't give me back my watch!"

I didn't know what to say. I couldn't believe we had just stolen Alistair's watch only to find out that it didn't work.

Alistair stared at his watch for a moment, and then tore it off his wrist. "What's the point of *having* this Blaronite technology if I'm not allowed to use it?" He dangled the watch over the storm-drain opening, threatening to drop it down to the sewer.

"Hey!" I grabbed the watch from Alistair's hand. "We'd really be in trouble if this got lost!"

Alistair sighed. "I know. You're right."

"We'll get Shirley out of there somehow, Alistair," I promised as the two of us stood up and walked back toward Alistair's house.

"I'm not so sure. . . ." Alistair's voice trailed off because he was staring at something on the ground. "Take a look at this, Daniel," he said.

When I saw what Alistair was looking at, I started shouting and jumping around the yard. "It worked! It actually worked!!"

I could hardly believe it: Our slime mold had actually moved! It had found its way

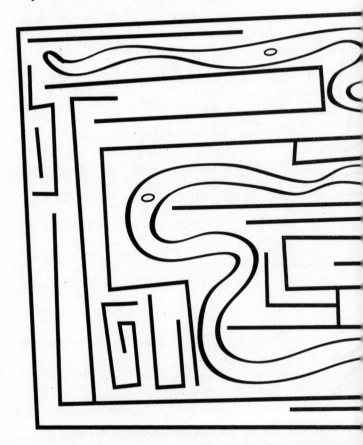

through the entire maze to the cookie!

In fact, I was so excited, I even volunteered to make our poster for the project. "This is going to be the best presentation ever!" I told Alistair.

Alistair nodded, but he didn't look so happy. I guessed our slime-mold success didn't exactly make up for our failed attempt to rescue Shirley.

26

A SHOCKING SUPRISE

AFTER SCHOOL, Alistair and I sat on the curb, staring at our slime mold.

"What do you think we should do with it now?" I asked.

It was late afternoon, and even though we were both still upset about not finding Shirley, even Alistair had to admit that our slime-mold presentation for Mr. Binns's class had been awesome.

"It was like the two of us were the stars of

our class for ten whole minutes!" Alistair said.

"I know," I agreed. "I loved how everyone said *EEEWWW!* when we showed them the slime mold for the first time."

"And then they all said 'NO WAY!' when we told them how the slime mold stretched itself through the maze," Alistair added

"But my favorite part was when then the whole class wanted to poke the slime mold with their fingers and scream," I said.

"I thought that part was a little annoying," Alistair admitted. "I don't think Chauncey liked our presentation."

"He was just jealous because Mr. Binns was giving us so many compliments," I said.

Alistair tapped a bunch of random buttons on his watch, but none of them worked. "Too bad I won't be doing any more presentations on Earth."

"Of course you will," I said.

Alistair shook his head. "Not if I can't get

Shirley out of the sewer." Alistair sighed and stared up at the sky as if he expected to see the Bumblepod hovering above us.

That's when a flash of light caught my attention. It was something on Alistair's watch.

"Hey, Alistair!" I said. "I think your dad forgot to deactivate one of your watch functions!"

Alistair gasped; his watch flashed and beeped.

ARE YOU SURE YOU WANT TO ACTIVATE THE INSTA-MONSTER RAY??

But before Alistair and I could decide what to do, we nearly fainted with surprise at the sound of Alistair's dad running across the front yard and yelling at us: "Alistair! You do *not* have permission to use your watch! Wait until your mother hears about this!"

"Dad," Alistair began, "let me explain—"

But Alistair's dad didn't wait for an explanation; he lunged forward to grab Alistair's watch.

At the same moment, Alistair tried to jump to his feet. This caused Alistair to bump into his dad, which caused Alistair's dad to trip over the our slime-mold maze.

The next thing we knew, the insta-monster ray shot from Alistair's watch, blasting both Alistair's dad and the slime mold at the same time!

In an instant, Alistair's dad and the slime mold merged into the strangest creature that has ever crawled across either Earth or Planet Blaron.

27

A BAD DAY FOR BEANIE

THEN IGGY AND DOTTIE ran out of our house. They both screamed when they saw a hideous monster in their front yard.

"I'm sorry, Dad!" Alistair shouted as he frantically pushed buttons on his watch, trying to reverse what had just happened. But the rest of the watch was still dead.

It seemed that Alistair's dad could no longer hear any of us. In the spot where Alistair's dad used to be there was only a giant, yellow-green, squishy slime-mold monster that had more eyeballs than I could count.

For a moment, I worried that the monster would attack us, but instead, it tried to escape by squeezing itself into the storm drain.

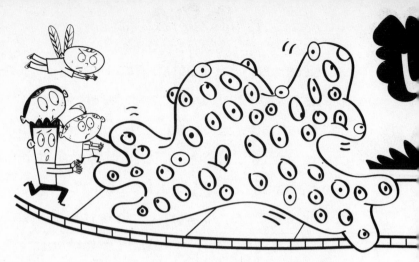

"Don't let him get away!" Alistair shouted.

Iggy quickly sprouted wings and dive-bombed the slime-mold monster with his stinger!

Instead of fighting Iggy, the monster rolled itself into a ball and bounced down the sidewalk.

"Follow my dad!" Alistair shouted, pointing at the slime-mold monster. "Don't let him get away!"

The four of us followed the monster as he slithered, stretched, and bounced his way through the neighborhood.

Farther up the street, I spied Beanie sitting on the sidewalk, chained to a parking meter. The little dog jumped to his feet and growled when he saw the slime-mold monster, a winged

boy, and three other kids stampeding toward him.

Everything happened so fast. In the blink of an eye, the monster snatched Beanie right off his leash!

Iggy tried to dive-bomb Alistair's dad with his wasp stinger again, but he couldn't make the monster let go of Beanie.

"Stingers can't hurt him, Iggy!" Alistair shouted. "We'll have to think of something else!"

"Like what?" I asked.

But before Alistair could answer, the monster opened his gaping slime-mold mouth and dropped Beanie inside!

We couldn't believe it: *Beanie was gone!*

THE PET THIEF

AS IT TURNED OUT, the slime-mold monster didn't exactly *eat* Beanie. We knew the little dog was alive because we could still see him, trapped and whimpering

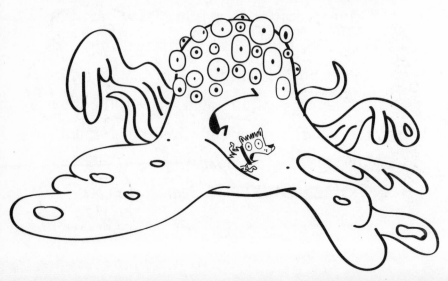

inside what looked like a little cage made of slime mold on the monster's back.

"DON'T WORRY, BEANIE!" Dottie shouted. "WE GOING SAVE YOU!"

"Dad!" Alistair shouted. "Let that dog go! Blaronites don't have pets!"

But there was no reasoning with Alistair's dad now that he had turned into a pet-snatching monster. As Alistair's monster-dad slithered, stretched, rolled, and bounced his way through the neighborhood, he kidnapped every pet he saw!

He grabbed a goldfish from an apartment window. . . .

He scooped up cats napping on the side-walk. . . .

He snatched dogs off their leashes, right from under their owners' noses!

He hoisted a pot-bellied pig from its home. . . .

He unloaded a rabbit family from its hutch. . . .

He stole a guinea pig from a school class-room. . . .

He shook squirrels from the trees!

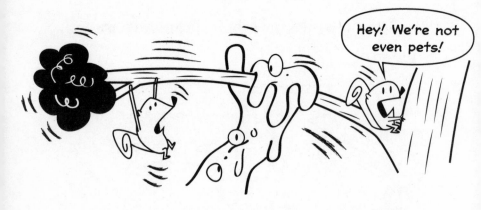

Hey! We're not even pets!

By now, the monster was a slithering, sliding, slime-mold-and-eyeball-covered jail for kidnapped pets. No matter how much the trapped animals howled, mewed, barked, bit, hissed, and scratched, Alistair's monster-dad refused to let them go.

And no matter how many pets the monster stole, he always had room for a few more.

Finally, we caught up with Alistair's dad and his collection of kidnapped pets at the corner of one of the busiest streets in town.

"Dad!" Alistair shouted. "You have to listen to me!"

But instead of listening, the monster bounced across four lanes of traffic, almost causing several accidents as he darted between cars.

"DAD!" Alistair yelled, "COME BACK!"

But it was too late: The monster darted into an alley and disappeared from our sight.

29

WATER-BUG RESCUE

ALISTAIR, Iggy, Dottie, and I walked to a nearby park and sat on a bench to rest for a minute while we thought about what we should do next.

All over we saw signs posted by people searching for lost pets:

LOST DOG!
Baffled Owner offers
REWARD!

LOST CAT!
ANSWERS TO THE NAME
MISS FLUFFY

LOST GOLDFISH!
How the heck do you lose a goldfish???

LOST POT-BELLED PIG
Answers to the name Princess Poinky!

Sniffling kids and worried adults were calling for their lost dogs, cats, rabbits, pigs, and guinea pigs.

"Our goal was to rescue one animal," Alistair said, "and instead, a whole neighborhood of pets has been kidnapped."

Alistair and I just sat there feeling bad as we listened to all those pet-sad people searching for their animals in the park.

I noticed clouds gathering overhead and I felt a cold drop of rain.

Where is Alistair's dad right now? I wondered. *And what will happen to Alistair and his family now that Alistair's dad is a slime-mold monster?*

As another raindrop fell on my cheek, I realized it was time to face the truth: *Commander Stickyfoot will probably send Alistair back to Planet Blaron when he finds out what happened to Alistair's dad.*

Nearby, Iggy and Dottie were throwing pebbles and leaves into a shallow stream where a trickle of dirty water flowed from a large storm overflow pipe.

I watched as Dottie began jumping from one stepping-stone to another toward the storm overflow pipe.

Iggy followed her, but he lost his footing and his feet got wet.

"IGGY!" I yelled, "Get out of the water!"

"OKAY, DANO!"

I was surprised to hear Iggy say "Okay" without arguing. But a moment later, I was amazed that Iggy had figured out a way to "get out of" the water while still staying *on top of it.*

I blinked, trying to make sure my eyes weren't playing tricks on me: *Iggy had sprouted extra legs—water-bug legs—that enabled him to skitter across the surface of the stream!*

I watched Iggy run across the stream like a giant water bug. Suddenly he stopped moving. Frozen, he stared down into the water.

I heard a *SPLASH!* as Iggy grabbed for something in the water.

"Can you believe that, Alistair?" I said, pointing at Iggy. "Now Iggy has *water-bug* traits, and he just used his pincers to catch a minnow!"

Alistair seemed weirdly distracted. He stood very still, as if listening to some secret message. "Daniel," Alistair said, "I have a feeling that Shirley is close by."

"That doesn't make sense. Shirley's down in the sewer, and we're at a park."

Alistair pointed to a large cement storm-water pipe by the stream. "That storm pipe might lead us to her."

Alistair waded through the stream, toward the overflow pipe. "Follow me to that pipe, everyone!" Alistair shouted. "And bring that fish you caught, Iggy!"

At the storm-water pipe we peered inside what looked like a metal tunnel that was wide enough for Iggy and Dottie to walk through easily. Alistair and I would have to stoop over to move through it. It was starting to rain so we were happy to go inside.

"SHIRLEY?" Alistair called, ducking his head and taking a step inside. "I just know she's in here," Alistair whispered. "We have a chance of finding her here if we go in deeper and explore."

"Okay, Awistair!" Iggy zoomed ahead fearlessly walking along the wall with his water-bug legs, which was actually a pretty freaky thing to see.

Raindrops clattered on the outer surface of the storm-water pipe as we splashed our way through shallow, dirty water on the floor. Soon we couldn't hear the rain anymore, and Alistair said we must be walking underground, beneath the houses and streets of our neighborhood.

"Alistair," I whispered, "I keep thinking about this scary movie about a bunch of kids who have the dumb idea of playing in a storm drain. The kids end up getting trapped when a thunderstorm hits and then the overflow pipe fills with water, and I think one of them ends up drowning. . . ."

Alistair put his hand on my shoulder. "Listen!" he said. We heard a splashing sound from the darkness.

"Hey!" Iggy called from farther down the pipe, "Der's a ladder here!"

When we caught up with Iggy, we found a landing with enough space for Alistair and me to stand up straight. There were two ladders: one led up to a manhole overhead, and the other led down into the deep, dark sewer water below.

"We must be under one of the main streets in town," Alistair guessed.

That's when I noticed that the water level below seemed to be rising. *It must be raining pretty hard outside if the sewer is filling with water that quickly*, I thought, feeling more worried.

Alistair waved his watch flashlight over the dark water below. "Shirley? Are you there? It's me, Alistair!"

Something snaked and wriggled beneath the dirty water—*something that reminded me of a giant sea intestine.*

"Alistair, look!" I pointing toward the water, "It's her!"

"Hang on, Shirley!" Alistair scrambled down the ladder toward the dark water below. "We're going to take you home!"

Alistair stood on a rung of the ladder just

above the surface of the water, but he still couldn't reach Shirley. She was too far away and too deep below the surface.

"Iggy!" Alistair said, "I need your help!"

"OKAY, AWISTAIR!" Iggy shouted, using his bug legs to walk straight down the wall and onto the water. "I GET HER!"

Iggy tiptoed across the surface of the sewer water until he reached Shirley.

"That's right, Iggy," Alistair said, lowering his voice. "Offer her that minnow you caught as bait . . . And when she bites it, *grab* her!"

We all held our breath, watching as Iggy waited for Shirley to grab the minnow.

Then, with the perfect timing of a giant water bug attacking its meal, Iggy grabbed Shirley and held her tightly in his pincers!"

"TA-DA!" Iggy shouted. "I HODING HAGGIE-BABY!!! And I NOT going flush you dis time, Haggie!"

Dottie jumped up and down. "Hooray for Iggy!"

Alistair gave Iggy the biggest smile I had seen since the day he lost Shirley.

Unfortunately, the four of us weren't able to celebrate Shirley's rescue for long.

30

OUT OF THE SHADOWS

ALISTAIR suddenly fell silent. "We're not alone," he whispered, pointing toward something that lurked in the shadows.

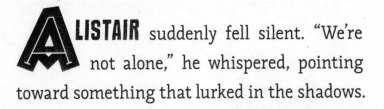

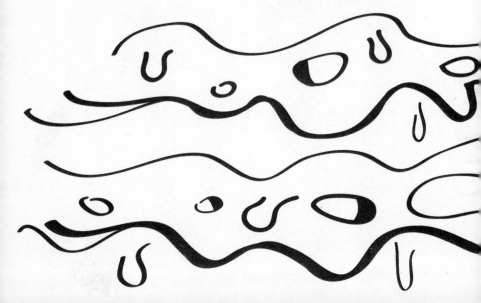

Then I saw it too: hundreds of slimy tentacles covered an entire cement wall. They stretched toward us, moving faster and faster!

"Alistair," I said, "you don't think your dad would—"

"I hope not," Alistair replied. "I mean, I seriously hope not."

We both had a feeling of dread. *Had the slime-mold monster slithered into the sewer to kidnap the one pet Alistair's dad hates more than any other pet in the entire world—a hagfish called Shirley?*

· 31 ·

BATTLING THE SEWER MONSTER

SPLASH! The monster sprung from the cement wall into the rising sewer water, then headed right for Iggy and Shirley! The terrified pets still trapped on the monster's slimy back howled and whined at the black water surrounding them.

"GET OUT OF THERE, IGGY!" Alistair, Dottie, and I shouted. "HURRY!"

Iggy tried to scurry out of the water and back up the wall, but the monster was faster. It grabbed one of Iggy's bug legs!

Iggy fought back, biting and pinching the monster!

But the monster hardly noticed Iggy's stinging attack. Instead, he stretched a slime-mold hand toward Iggy and Shirley and then squeezed the two of them together in a tight fist.

It was when the monster tried to stuff Iggy and Shirley into one of its slime-mold cages that he got the surprise of his life: *hagfish slime!*

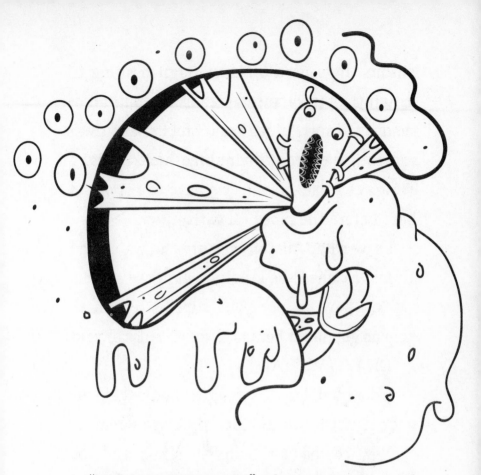

"YAY FOR SHIRLEY!" Alistair, Dottie, and I cheered. "Hooray for hagfish slime!"

"That's the key, Iggy!" Alistair shouted, "This monster can't handle hagfish slime; it's your most powerful weapon! Now use the hagfish slime to free the other animals!"

"OKAY, AWISTAIR!"

Hanging on to Shirley with his water-bug

pincers, Iggy used Shirley's hagfish slime to loosen the sticky animal traps and pull all of the dogs, cats, guinea pigs, rabbits, and even squirrels free from their slime-mold cages.

"Iggy," Alistair said, "we have to get out of here before the pipes fill with water."

I saw what Alistair meant: The water had almost reached the landing where we stood.

"You have to use your super-strength to help us get out of here fast, Iggy!" Alistair said.

"OKAY, AWISTAIR!"

I doubted Iggy's strength would help us get out of the storm pipe, but I was wrong.

Now coated with hagfish slime and too slippery to stick to anything it touched, the slime-mold monster was like a helpless lump of dough in Iggy's hands. Iggy put his super-strength to work. He squished, punched, and squeezed the slime-mold monster into some-thing completely new: a monster waterslide that sent everyone on a wild ride through the storm pipe!

PUNCH!

SQUEEZE!

We all slipped and slid all the way through
the storm-water pipe and back into the stream!

Everyone except Iggy and Dottie thought the "pet-party slide" was terrifying.

Once we were all safely outside the storm-water pipe, Alistair found an old bucket to carry Shirley and filled it with water.

The exhausted slime-mold monster now lay on the ground like a giant puddle as dazed animals sniffed around the edges of the stream and licked bits of mud from their matted fur.

"Now what?" I asked Alistair.

Before he could answer, a familiar bright light surrounded Alistair, Iggy, Dottie, me, Alistair's monster-dad, and Shirley.

I felt a tickle under my skin and then the weightless feeling that meant we were about to get transported into outer space.

· 32 ·

ALISTAIR'S PRIZE

ALISTAIR, Iggy, Dottie, and I were on board the Spaceship Bumblepod. Alistair's bucket containing Shirley sat next to him. Alistair's dad was also there, and we were relieved to see that he was back in his human disguise again. I guessed Commander Stickyfoot and Miss Bubbles had used their Blaronite technology to reverse the effects of the "insta-monster" ray from Alistair's watch.

"You've made some huge mistakes, Alistair," Commander Stickyfoot began.

"I know," Alistair said.

"But—" Commander Stickyfoot continued, "every once in a blue frackenpoy, the benefits of a particular mistake outweigh its drawbacks."

Alistair looked up, surprised.

Alistair's dad also looked surprised, but he was also angry. "With all due respect, Commander Stickyfoot," he said, "I see *zero* benefits to Alistair's mistakes."

Alistair hung his head and looked down at the table.

Mr. Stickyfoot and Miss Bubbles whispered something to each other.

"Alistair's dad," Miss Bubbles began, "since you've been in monster form during the past few hours, you might not be aware of a crisis that happened here on the Bumblepod today."

"What crisis?" Now Alistair and his dad *both* looked surprised.

"Following Alistair's last visit aboard the Bumblepod, Miss Bubbles took an interest in this Earth species called the hagfish and began secretly studying it during her spare time."

"She did?!" Alistair was shocked.

"And a good thing she did, too," Commander Stickyfoot continued, "because just a few hours ago, the Bumblepod was caught in an unexpected meteor shower that damaged our most important equipment. At first, we thought the damage to our controls couldn't be repaired without returning to Planet Blaron and abandoning our Earth surveillance mission. But then Miss Bubbles had a unusual idea."

We all looked at Miss Bubbles, wondering what this "unusual idea" was.

"Hagfish slime!" Miss Bubbles shouted.

"Hagfish slime?!" Alistair's dad looked disgusted.

"Yes!" Miss Bubbles continued. "Because hagfish slime is one of the strongest natural fibers in the universe, it made the perfect material for our repairs to the Bumblepod!"

"So," Alistair said, glancing sideways at his dad, "you're saying that having a pet hagfish turned out to be a *good* thing?"

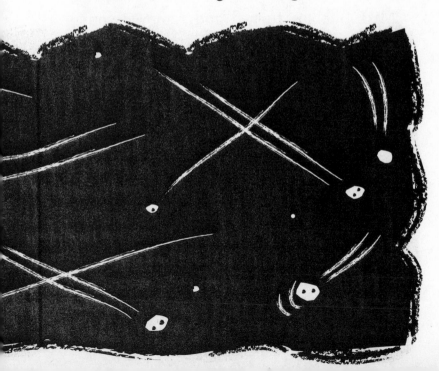

"It turned out to be a *great* thing," Commander Stickyfoot replied. "In fact, hagfish slime is one of the most useful resources we've encountered through your Earth mission."

Alistair grinned at his dad.

"And Alistair," Commander Stickyfoot added, "to honor your contribution to the Blaronite mission, we have summoned you here today to give you a special prize."

"AWISTAIR GETTING A PRIZE?" Iggy shouted. "I WANTS A PRIZE, TOO!!"

"Shush, Iggy," I said.

Miss Bubbles turned and removed something from a box. We all craned our necks to see Alistair's prize.

Alistair looked thrilled as Miss Bubbles placed the prize on his head.

Iggy, Dottie, and I couldn't believe it. A crown made of broccoli was pretty much the worst prize we had ever seen. I felt terrible for Alistair, but he seemed pretty happy.

I raised my hand. "Um, does this mean Alistair gets to stay on planet Earth?"

"Under a few conditions," Mr. Stickyfoot said.

"Don't tell me," Alistair said. "No pets. Right?"

"It's actually homework for you and your dad, Alistair," Commander Stickyfoot said.

Alistair's dad groaned. He reminded me of the kids in Mr. Binns's class when Mr. Binns tells us we have a new book report due.

Alistair didn't look too thrilled about the "homework" idea either.

But at least Alistair and his dad will still be on planet Earth. I felt a huge sense of relief, just knowing that my best friend would be around.

· 33 ·

AFTERWORD

AFTER ALISTAIR received his award from Commander Stickyfoot, he spent several days taking care of Shirley in her aquarium. During this time, Alistair says he was able to "listen" to his pet and better understand what she needed.

"She was telling me she missed the ocean," he said. "She was telling me she missed a life of adventures and gnawing on dead whales on the ocean floor."

So once Shirley was strong enough, Alistair took her back to the ocean and set her free.

"It's funny," Alistair said after releasing Shirley into the water, "Shirley is gone, but I don't feel the terrible pet sadness I had when she was lost in the sewer."

"Maybe that's because you know she's happy now," I said. "Instead of losing her, you can feel happy that you rescued her and set her free."

And in case you're wondering about that "homework" for Alistair and his dad, here's what it is:

Once a week, Alistair and his dad have to conduct what Alistair calls "a very uncomfortable experiment"—the Earth tradition known as "father-son playtime."

Alistair told me that their homework started going better after his dad figured out that his human disguise makes him really uncomfortable.

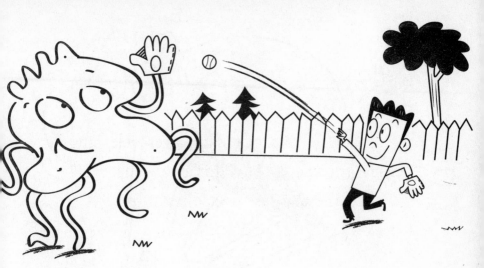

Lately, the two of them have a lot more fun when they play outside in Alistair's back-yard where Alistair's dad is free to just be his baggy Blaronite self.

It's true that when Alistair's dad isn't wearing his human disguise, he looks a little freaky. But he can do so many cool things!

In fact, Alistair's dad is so much happier these days, he might even let Alistair get a new pet!

"But this time I'll look for a more traditional Earth pet that doesn't mind living in captivity," Alistair said. "It has to be something cute, of course—maybe a tarantula named Shirley."

I told Alistair that after having a hagfish for a pet, a tarantula sounded like a great idea.

ACKNOWLEDGMENTS

I want to thank the wonderful publishing team at Penguin for their hard work on *Iggy Loomis* and also for their friendship and the opportunities to develop as a writer and to connect with so many readers and educators! In particular I appreciate all the fabulous insights from Lucia Monfried, which helped make Iggy and his adventures come to life. Many thanks also to Lauri Hornik, Stacey Friedberg, Rosanne Lauer, Jason Henry, and Doug Stewart for countless contributions to this book as well as other projects for young readers. Finally, thank you to my family for so much inspiration, for making me laugh, and for always being my favorite readers.

. YOU WILL ALSO LIKE .

IGGY LOOMIS
SUPERKID IN TRAINING

Illustrated
··· by ···
MIKE
MORAN

· JENNIFER ALLISON ·